WILLIAM WENTON

LURIMET TYVEN

BOBBIE PEERS

Translated from Norwegian by Tara Chace

**WALKER
BOOKS**

This translation has been published with the financial support of NORLA

First published in Great Britain 2017 by Walker Books Ltd
87 Vauxhall Walk, London SE11 5HJ

Published by agreement with Salomonsson Agency

2 4 6 8 10 9 7 5 3 1

Text © 2015 Bobbie Peers
Originally published as *Luridiumstyven* by Aschehoug
English translation by Tara Chace © 2017 Salomonsson Agency
Cover illustration by Nikolai Lockertsen

This book has been typeset in Adobe Garamond Pro

Printed and bound in Great Britain by Clays Ltd, St Ives plc

British Library Cataloguing in Publication Data:
a catalogue record for this book is available from the British Library

ISBN 978-1-4063-7170-3

www.walker.co.uk

*For Michelle: had it not been for you,
this book would never have been*

Victoria Station, London

It was the middle of the morning rush hour. Busy, harried people scurried this way and that, everyone minding their own business. No one noticed an elderly bearded man running through the hall. He was clutching a brown-paper parcel and kept looking behind him, as if he was being chased.

He stumbled on a suitcase that someone was wheeling by. It took him a few steps to catch his balance, then he hurtled down the escalator to the underground.

Down on the platform, people were crushed together like lemmings on a cliff. The man pushed his way through and stopped at the far end of the platform. A cool breeze blew out of the tunnel. A train was coming.

None of the other travellers noticed the man jump down onto the tracks. The screech of an approaching train could be heard, and the wind whistling through the tunnel made his long beard flap.

The old man cast one last look up the platform before he turned and disappeared into the dark tunnel.

CHAPTER 1

Eight years later, at a secret address somewhere in Norway

William was so engrossed in what he was doing that he didn't hear his mother calling him. He sat hunched over a massive desk, and with a steady hand he tightened the final screw into a metal cylinder the size of an empty toilet roll. The cylinder, which divided into several sections, was engraved with intricate symbols and inscriptions.

William held it up to the light and studied it with satisfaction. He picked up a newspaper clipping, which showed a picture of a cylinder that looked just like the one he was holding in his hand. It said: *The Impossible Puzzle, the world's most difficult code, is coming to Norway. Can you crack it?*

Even though William had already read the article hundreds of times, he read it again. He studied the picture of the enigmatic metal cylinder. A group of the world's best cryptographers had spent more than three years creating it. And now it was on its introductory tour with the tagline "the world's most difficult code". It was reputed to be impossible to crack. Some of the world's smartest people had already tried – and failed. And now it had finally come to Norway. Soon he would see it with his own eyes. He could hardly wait. Tomorrow the exhibition was moving on to Finland, so it was now or never.

"DINNER!" William's mother yelled from the kitchen.

William didn't respond. In his defence, sound did not travel particularly well in this house. The walls of every room were covered in bookshelves jam-packed with books that had been inherited from his grandfather, along with strict instructions never to get rid of them. The collection had been hauled over from England in seven large containers.

William had read them all. At least twice.

It had been eight years since they'd had to leave England. Eight years since they'd moved into this house. And eight years since Grandfather had disappeared. Now William and his parents lived incognito at a secret address, with new names, in a small town in Norway.

"WILLIAM OLSEN! DINNER!"

His mother didn't let up. William heard her now. She had said *Olsen*, William Olsen. He was never going to get used to that name. He longed for the day when he could tell everyone his actual name: William Wenton.

He'd given up asking about what really happened back in London eight years earlier. About why they were called Olsen now. About why they lived here, in Norway of all places. And about what had happened to his grandfather. His parents had decided not to talk about it. As if all the secrets were somehow better than the truth.

He didn't know much about what had happened, except that it had something to do with a car accident. The same car accident that had left his father paralysed.

But there was more. Something so serious that his family had to disappear – and a thin little country that almost no one in the rest of the world could find on a map had been the perfect place to disappear to.

"DIIIINNER!!" his mum yelled yet again.

"I just have to fix one little thing…" William muttered to himself. Then it was his father's turn to holler from the distance: "WILLIAM … IT'S TIME FOR DINNER!"

William cautiously rotated the metal cylinder, feeling how the small pieces rested perfectly in his hands as if they understood him. Then the door to his room suddenly flew open, knocking over a tall stack of books. He jumped. One of the books hit the cylinder, which slipped out of his hands, landed on the floor with a *clunk!* and began to roll towards the door. William was just leaning down to pick it up when his father came over the threshold in his electric wheelchair, on a collision course with the cylinder. William watched in dismay as the full weight of one wheel drove over it with a metallic *crunch!* His father braked abruptly. The ruined electronics sparked and a little cloud of smoke rose from the wreckage under the wheel. His father glared down at his wheelchair in irritation and wrinkled his nose.

"Is it playing up again? I just took it in to get it serviced!" he muttered to himself and then turned sternly towards William, who had moved his hand to cover the newspaper clipping on the desk. "It's time for dinner … NOW!" said his father, putting his chair in reverse, bumping into another stack of books and driving back out of the room.

William waited until the hum of his father's stairlift had faded before he stood up. He took a breath. That had been close. But his father hadn't seen anything, had he? William was quite sure that he'd managed to hide the newspaper clipping before his father noticed it. He walked over to the cylinder and picked it up. One side was dented. He shook it gently.

"Really?" He was annoyed with himself as much as anything. He glanced at the thick safety chain on the inside of his door. How had he forgotten to fasten it? He always locked his door when he was working on codes.

William turned and walked back over to the desk. He opened one of the drawers and put into it the newspaper clipping and what was left of the cylinder. He stood there for a while, staring thoughtfully at the other objects in the drawer: a mechanical hand he'd built himself, a 3-D metal puzzle, a Rubik's cube and a shoebox that contained a soldering iron, some small screwdrivers and a pair of pliers.

He closed the drawer and locked it, hiding the key in a crack between two floorboards, then gave the room one last check to make sure he'd stowed everything away.

For some reason his father hated cryptography. In fact he'd forbidden any form of codebreaking activity. He wanted William to do the stuff normal children did: football, band practice, whatever. It was almost as if his father was afraid of codes, and afraid of William's interest in them. And it was getting worse. Now his dad was even cutting the crossword puzzles out of the newspaper and burning them in the fireplace. That's why William had started locking his bedroom door. So his father wouldn't discover all the stuff he had hidden in his room.

If his father only knew what it was like to be William. Some days all he could see around him were codes. For him, anything could be a code: a house, a car, stuff he saw on TV or read in a book. They were all puzzles, and his brain took over to solve them. It could even happen when he looked at a tree or the pattern in some wallpaper. Sometimes it was as if things dissolved right before his eyes so that he could see each individual component and where it fitted in. He'd had this gift for as long as he could remember, and it often got him into trouble. That's why he was happiest on his own. Preferably in his room, with the door locked, where he was in full control.

William looked again at the big desk; his grandfather's desk. The top was made from dark ebony, one of the hardest woods in the world. In each corner there were carvings of demon-like faces, grimacing and sticking out their tongues.

William had been scared of the desk when he was little. But gradually, as he got older, he became curious. The whole desk top was covered with strange symbols. William imagined that they were secret messages from his grandfather, who was one of the best cryptologists in the world. Only, William hadn't managed to decipher the symbols yet. He hoped that someday he would understand them, that he would understand what his grandfather had written, and why.

"WE'RE EATING NOW!" His mother yelled again.

"Coming!" William replied. And in two easy steps he was out of the room.

CHAPTER 2

"Aren't you hungry?" his mother asked.

"Not really," William responded, pushing his plate away.

His father swallowed his mouthful. "You sit around too much," he said. "When I was your age, we never just sat around. We played football, ran around outside, stole fruit off the neighbours' trees. Look at you – you're skin and bones."

William tried to ignore his dad, but he knew he was right. He *was* skin and bones. But he was stronger than he looked. He always had been. No one in his class could do more push-ups than him. Even William's PE teacher had trouble keeping up with him when he got going.

William glanced at the folded newspaper and pair of scissors sitting in his dad's lap. Recently his father had started cutting even more out of the newspaper than the crossword – ever since advertisements had started appearing about the Impossible Puzzle exhibition that was coming to the History of Science Museum. His father seemed to be trying as hard as he could to keep William away from it.

But what his father didn't know was that William's class was planning a trip to see the exhibition. His mum had told William he could go if he promised not to say anything to his father. And didn't touch any of the artefacts. It was as if his mum understood how much it meant to him, as if she recognized the tingle William felt every time he thought about the code no one had been able to crack, as if his mum knew he'd been dreaming about the exhibition ever since he'd first heard of the Impossible Puzzle. As if she knew, too, that it was now or never.

After his dad had left the table, William and his mother sat for a few more minutes. "Mr Turnbull is very concerned about the trip to the museum tomorrow," said his mum. "And so am I, actually. Living in hiding for so long has been hard for all of us, but we really can't draw attention to ourselves. You do know that, don't you?"

William didn't respond. He was thinking about his teacher, Mr Turnbull, who had hated him ever since William had corrected him in class one day.

"Look at me, William," his mum said sternly.

He turned and looked at her.

"Promise me you're going to behave yourself tomorrow!" she pleaded. "Can you promise me that? We've got to keep a low profile."

William knew he was going to have a hard time keeping his

hands off the Impossible Puzzle. But he also knew he couldn't do anything that would give them away.

"I promise," he said and felt a twinge in his stomach.

CHAPTER 3

"Hello, and welcome to the History of Science Museum," said the tall, nervous-looking woman who greeted them outside the museum. It looked as if she had been waiting for a while. Her nose was as red as a tomato and she was shivering. She jumped up and down to keep warm while Mr Turnbull tried to get the class to settle down. "My name is Edna and I'll be your guide today. We have an exciting afternoon planned!" She nervously straightened her skirt. "You've arrived a little later than expected, which means that unfortunately it will not be possible to visit the Impossible Puzzle exhibition. But of course you have the whole of the rest of the museum to explore."

William stiffened. They were too late? It couldn't be true.

"Since you didn't quite make it to see the Impossible Puzzle, we'll start instead with the science word puzzles. Everyone should take a sheet of paper from the table just inside the doors there," said Edna. "It'll work best if you do it in pairs."

It only took a few seconds for the students to team up with

their usual partners. William was still frozen to the spot, paralysed with disappointment.

"Come on, William, we don't have all day," Mr Turnbull chided.

William nodded vaguely. Then his anger flared. Word puzzles? No way. He was here to see the Impossible Puzzle!

"We'll meet by the exit in one hour," squeaked Edna, opening the large oak front doors of the museum.

As the class traipsed noisily up the front steps, one of the girls bumped into Edna, knocking her down. The guide sat on the step, dazed. Mr Turnbull rushed towards her and she held out her arm so he could help her up.

But Mr Turnbull hurried right past. "No running … WALK!" he yelled at the top of his lungs, and kept going into the museum without so much as looking at her.

William stopped in front of Edna, took her hand and helped her up.

"Thank you," she said, brushing off her skirt.

"You're welcome," said William meekly. He hesitated a moment. "Is the Impossible Puzzle exhibition completely shut?" he asked.

"They're at maximum capacity down there. We can't let anyone else in – fire regulations," Edna said.

William nodded and carried on through the doors.

The first thing he noticed as he entered the museum was two men taking down a poster next to a staircase. It said:

Impossible Puzzle Exhibition – downstairs.

He glanced over at Mr Turnbull, who was already busy with a boy whose hand had got stuck in a steam engine. A museum guard had come over to help.

William smiled. Mr Turnbull had his hands full. Now was his chance to get into the Impossible Puzzle exhibition.

CHAPTER 4

William walked down the stairs and stopped. Two enormous guards in grey uniforms were blocking the doorway to what was clearly the Impossible Puzzle exhibition. People were packed into the room beyond like sardines. One of the guards was trying to placate an angry little man who obviously wanted to enter. The man waved his ticket under the guard's nose.

"I've already paid. You can't refuse to let me in if I have a ticket," he yelled.

"Then you should have been here earlier. We can't let any more people in. The exhibition is at maximum capacity." The guard pointed at the crowd behind him to emphasize his point.

"Look at me. I'm only four foot nine. I weigh fifty kilos. No one is going to notice if I'm out here or in there," the man argued.

"Sorry," the other guard said firmly, folding his arms across his chest.

The little man stood there for a few seconds. William saw

him clenching his hands into fists like a stubborn four-year-old. His face became redder and redder, as if he was about to explode.

Then he turned around and headed back up the stairs. William walked over to the guards.

"Excuse me," he said as innocently as he could. The two men glanced down at him.

"I'm here with my class and we're supposed to be in there," he said, pointing into the exhibition.

"Is the rest of your class in there?" one of the guards asked.

"Um … yeah," William lied.

"Do you have a stamp?"

William was about to say something when a figure suddenly came flying through the air and hit one of the guards with a *smack!*

"LET ME IN! LET ME IN! LET ME IN!" The little man was now hanging around the guard's neck and trying to climb over his head to enter the exhibition.

"Get him off me, Svein!" the guard yelled. "Get him off!"

The other guard grabbed the man's legs and tried to pull him off his colleague, but he clung to the guard's neck like an angry octopus.

"He's stronger than he looks, Håvard. Tickle him under the arms – make him let go!" yelled the first guard.

"Tickle him yourself!" the other guard shouted back, his arms flailing.

Several other guards arrived to help. None of them noticed William slip through the open doors behind them.

Soon William was standing in the middle of a large room, surrounded by people. He felt a familiar tingle in his body. He had to find a spot where he could get a good view. It was only a question of time before Mr Turnbull discovered that he was missing, and once he had he would move heaven and earth to find him. The Impossible Puzzle exhibition would be the first place he'd check.

"Only five minutes left to decipher the world's most difficult puzzle!" a voice announced over the PA system. "Many have tried, but none have succeeded. Yet."

William glanced around. On the wall at the far end of the room he spotted a screen on which large, red numbers were counting down. A poster with a picture of the Impossible Puzzle was hanging over the countdown clock. William pushed his way forward. He didn't have any plans to solve the Impossible Puzzle. He just wanted to see it. Preferably when someone else was trying to solve it. His pulse sped up, adrenaline pumped.

A couple of minutes later, William had managed to worm his way through the crowd and was standing in front of a small stage.

Onstage were a chair and a table. A thin man in his midforties was sitting in the chair, his long, blond hair pulled back into a ponytail. He was leaning over the table, twisting sections of a metal cylinder. Beads of sweat appeared on his forehead. He was breathing hard, and regularly cast nervous glances up at the digital countdown clock on the wall above him.

A chubby man in a tight suit stood fidgeting nervously next to the table. William recognized him from TV. His name was Ludo Kläbbert and he was a well-known comedian and presenter. Ludo raised a microphone to his mouth and checked the clock before starting to count down.

"Ten … nine … eight … seven…"

Soon everyone in the room was counting with him. The long-haired man looked as if he was going to pass out.

"Five … four … three … two … one … zero!" cried Ludo. "Time's up! Have you solved it, Vektor Hansen?" Ludo looked at the sweaty man in the chair.

Vektor Hansen carefully set the cylinder down and shook his head in shame.

"Even Vektor Hansen, the man with the highest IQ in all of Norway, cannot solve the Impossible Puzzle. This truly is a tough nut to crack!" Ludo told the audience.

Suddenly Hansen stood up, and snatched the microphone from him.

"This is some kind of scam – a bad joke! There is no solution. It can't be solved," Vektor barked grumpily.

He picked up the Impossible Puzzle and raised it

threateningly over his head, as if he was about to smash it to the floor.

"This is nonsense!" he yelled.

Ludo waved over two uniformed guards, who hopped onto the stage, snatched the cylinder out of Vektor's grasp and handed it to Ludo before pulling Vektor down off the stage with them. A few people laughed, while others booed.

"I'm still a lot smarter than all of you put together!" yelled Hansen as he was ushered out of the door beside the stage. "You're all just a bunch of idiots. I'm a genius!" The door banged shut and it was quiet in the room.

Ludo stood onstage with the Impossible Puzzle in his hands. A murmur ran through the crowd.

"*Is* it just a trick?" a voice called out.

"Typical!" yelled someone else.

"No, no!" insisted Ludo.

"Prove it, then!" another voice called from the crowd. "Let one more person try!"

Ludo glanced nervously around. His eyes came to rest on a serious-looking woman with severe glasses who was standing next to the stage. She nodded.

"OK, but just one more. The time is actually up. Who wants to try?" cried Ludo, wiping the sweat off his forehead with the back of his hand.

The room fell completely silent. A couple of people murmured while others shook their heads.

"No one?" asked Ludo.

"William!" a loud voice suddenly called out.

William turned and saw Mr Turnbull pushing his way through the crowd and pointing at William, who was still standing in front of the stage.

And then everyone turned to look at William. "Yes, let him try it," someone said. The presenter looked at William in surprise.

"A kid? Why not? You never know." He gestured to William.

"No, wait!" yelled Mr Turnbull. "I didn't mean…"

But it was too late. Ludo had pulled William up on the stage and placed the Impossible Puzzle into his hands. William peered at the shiny cylinder. He couldn't believe his eyes.

"No, not—" said Mr Turnbull. He tried to make his way up onto the stage, but the guards held him back.

"Would you like to try?" Ludo asked William. "Some of the sharpest minds in the world have tried without succeeding."

William shook his head. "No, I don't think…"

"Oh, come on – it can't hurt to try," Ludo teased with a smile. He turned to the audience and limply waved a finger at them. "What do you say, folks? Would you like him to give it a try?"

The crowd broke into spontaneous applause.

William looked again at the Impossible Puzzle. He had never seen a single one of the symbols on the cylinder before. They weren't letters or numbers. But then something began to happen. The way it always did. It began in his stomach, like a warm ache. Then it spread up through his chest and out into his hands and his head. William tried to set the device down, to let go of it, but it was too late.

It was as if the small parts in the cylinder had come to life in his hands. Some of the pieces seemed to shrink, others changed colour. Some started glowing while others grew so dark that they almost disappeared. The symbols came loose from the cylinder and floated around his head like a swarm of butterflies. He followed them with his eyes. Then his hands began working. They twisted and turned the little components. His fingers moved faster and faster. *Click … click … click*, the device said.

Time and place ceased to exist.

It wasn't until a tremendous outburst of cheering practically raised the roof of the exhibition hall that William snapped out of his trance and looked down at the device he still held in his hands. But it was no longer a cylinder. It had split into two. And inside one half was engraved the word *CONGRATULATIONS!*

William couldn't speak. He just stared at the message inside the cylinder. His eyes saw what it said, but his brain refused to believe it. *It must be broken*, he thought. *I didn't solve it… I broke it.* He looked at Ludo, standing next to him, also speechless. Then he glanced at Mr Turnbull, who put his hands up to his head and collapsed onto the floor in front of the stage.

William tried to put the pieces back together, but it didn't work. He tried again. And again.

It must be broken. It MUST!

CHAPTER 5

The museum director's office was cramped. William was sitting in a chair in front of the director, who was studying the Impossible Puzzle. Journalists and other curious onlookers had gathered in the street outside. William could hear them yelling. The museum director kept turning the device over and over in his hand. He pulled out a magnifying glass, which he put to his eye. He brought the two puzzle pieces right up to his face.

"Hmm … hmm," he mumbled. "It doesn't look like it was prised open in any way." He regarded William over the top of his glasses.

William looked down at the floor, as if he'd done something wrong. And he had, of course. He'd promised his mother he wouldn't draw attention to himself.

"You realize we're going to have to speak to the media? People all over the world will want to know what you did," the museum director said.

All the colour drained from William's face.

"Is that really necessary?" he asked with a gulp.

This was a complete disaster. His mum was going to have a breakdown. And his dad…? William couldn't even begin to imagine how his father was going to react.

The museum director stared thoughtfully at William.

"You're under eighteen, so strictly speaking we need your parents' permission before we talk to the press. Could you give me your mum or dad's phone number?"

William squirmed in the chair and shook his head. "It would be best if I told them," he said. "My parents don't really like attention that much."

The museum director mulled that over for a moment and then shrugged. "All right, then," he said with a smile. "I'll have someone from the museum drive you home. You can sneak out the back way."

William stood up and moved towards the door.

"William," the museum director said. William stopped and turned around. "You know how incredible this is, right?"

A white delivery truck stopped at the end of the driveway. The door opened and William hopped out. He walked towards the house, took a deep breath as if he was about to dive under water, put his hand on the door handle and entered. He heard quiet voices coming from the living room.

His mother was sitting on the sofa and his father was next

to her in his wheelchair. The radio was on in the background. They looked up when William walked in but said nothing. The silence seemed to go on for ever.

"William," his father said finally, beckoning him over and turning up the volume on the radio.

"…and now back to the History of Science Museum and the sensational news about the Impossible Puzzle. This code, which up until today had been considered the hardest in the world, has now been deciphered. We still don't know the identity of the person who did it," the reporter said, "but we talked to someone who was there when it happened. And now over to you, Aslak."

His mother's hands were trembling. She clasped them together in her lap to try and calm them, but it didn't seem to help. William looked at the floor. He knew he was in serious trouble.

"Thank you. I'm standing here outside the History of Science Museum with Tordis Voffel, who was present when this amazing feat took place," the reporter announced. "Tordis, can you tell us what happened?"

A woman cleared her throat a couple of times before speaking. "I was there with my grandson. He likes codes and things like that. We were about to leave after that high-IQ guy had to give up. We wanted to beat the rush to the café – I'd promised Halvor I'd buy him an ice cream, chocolate, he's not that fond of—"

"And what happened then?" the interviewer interrupted impatiently.

"Well, suddenly there was a boy standing onstage," the woman said. "I don't know where he came from. He just appeared out of nowhere. I thought it was a bit strange that they would let a child try, especially after the other geniuses had to give up."

"And what happened?" the interviewer prompted.

"Before we knew it, he'd cracked the code! And then there was complete chaos in the room. I grabbed Halvor and pulled him out of there. I mean, you hear about people being trampled to death, and besides I had promised him I would..."

William's father turned off the radio and sat there for a moment without saying anything.

"Was it you?" he finally asked.

"I..." William began, but he couldn't get anything else out. His mother began to cry.

"It doesn't matter now. We have to pack!" his father said sharply, driving his wheelchair out of the room.

CHAPTER 6

William made his way up to the top of the house, then headed to the end of the the hallway. He ran his hand over the pinewood panelling on the wall. His forefinger stopped at a large knothole, wiggled its way inside and pressed something. There was a *click!* from inside the wall. Then the ceiling creaked and a trapdoor opened up above him.

He'd made the secret entrance himself.

William climbed up the ladder and disappeared through the opening into the attic. There was just enough room beneath the sloping roof for him to stand upright. Apart from one low bookshelf, the attic was almost empty, with just a few old cardboard boxes in one corner. William turned on a wall lamp and walked over to the bookshelf, which held a small number of volumes. These were the books that meant the most to him. William had no idea how many times he'd read them – hundreds, maybe. He knew them by heart. And what made it extra special was that they were full of his grandfather's notes. When he read them, he felt as if his grandfather was talking to him. He had learned so much from these books. Things you never heard about at school. He slid his fingers along the spines: *Secrets of the Cave Paintings*; *The Pyramids: The Largest Codes in the World*; *Atlantis: They Knew More Than We Do*; *The Earth Isn't What You Think.*

William sat down on the rug and pulled out a leather-bound photo album that was hidden beneath the shelf. He gently ran his finger over the first page. His grandfather's handwriting was just visible: *Excavation Documentation, Part 89.*

William slowly browsed through the album. He looked at the pictures his grandfather had taken at various archaeological digs. He had been everywhere. But William had no idea what he'd been looking for or what he'd found. Those were the kinds of questions he so wished he could ask his grandfather. There were pictures from all over the world: everything from famous places like the pyramids in Egypt to secret sites in the Amazon and Tibet. Next to the photographs, Grandfather had noted the places and the times, but never what they'd been looking for.

The ladder creaked. William looked up and saw his mother's head appear through the trapdoor. He closed the photo album.

"May I join you?" she asked.

William nodded.

His mum sat down next to him. She stayed there for a while with her hands in her lap.

William tried to find the words to express what he wanted to say, but he couldn't.

"There's so much you don't know. We wanted to protect you, didn't want you to walk around feeling scared," his mother began.

"What do you mean?" William asked.

"Your father and I … we've always known it couldn't last for ever. You're too much like your grandfather," she said, tousling William's hair. "I think it's time you knew what happened in London eight years ago." His mother swallowed drily. "The reason we're not safe."

"Are we in danger now?" he asked quietly.

"Yes, I think we are," she said.

They sat in silence for while. William was still holding the album. "Can I see?" his mum asked.

William nodded. His mum smiled at the sight of Grandfather's ornate handwriting.

"Time goes so quickly. It feels as if we saw him only yesterday."

She turned the first page. The next picture showed an overgrown Inca pyramid surrounded by thick jungle.

"Your grandfather loved his work. He was always on the go. But he loved his family, too. That's why he took such good care of you before he vanished. You meant the world to him, William."

"What happened to him?"

"We don't know for sure. He disappeared just after we moved to Norway."

"But why did we move?" William asked.

His mother looked at him. "It was to do with your grandfather's work. We don't know why, but he thought our lives were in danger and sent us here. We had to start a whole new life. No one could even know we were related to him. That's why we don't have any photos of him on the walls, and why we never say his name."

"But who's after us? And how can it be dangerous for people to find out that I solved a puzzle?"

"That wasn't just any old puzzle, William. It was the hardest one ever created. You and your grandfather are probably the only people in the world who could have done it. And now it's only a question of time before they find us." She turned to the next page in the album. The photo was of an old brass casing full of gears and levers. Under the picture in his grandfather's handwriting it said: *Computer, Greece. (Age: indefinite.)*

"There's one more thing..." His mum hesitated.

"What?" William asked.

"Well, you know your father doesn't like to talk about how he became paralysed..."

William nodded.

"But you know he was in a car accident?" his mother continued.

"Yes," said William.

"Well, he wasn't the only one in the car."

"*What?*"

"No," said his mother. "*You* were in the car with him."

"Me?" William's head began to swim.

"You barely survived. I thought you were going to die. That's what the doctors said – that you weren't going to make it." His mother wiped a tear from the corner of her eye.

"So how did I survive?" asked William, his voice quavering.

His mum glanced down at the photo album. She was quiet for what seemed like an eternity.

"Your grandfather was out of the country, working. When he heard about the accident, he caught the first flight home. He sat by your bedside every night for weeks ... and then you suddenly started to improve. The doctors didn't know what was going on. Your grandfather said it was a miracle."

William tried to put his thoughts in order. He had almost died? And his grandfather had watched over him ... and then he'd recovered?

He glanced back up at his mother, and saw how she was trembling.

"Mum, who are we hiding from?" he asked. "Does it have anything to do with the accident?"

"I don't know, William," she said and stood up.

"But..." William began, then stopped. It was clear that his mother didn't want to talk more.

"We're leaving tomorrow. It isn't safe for us here any more."

"Where are we going?" William asked.

"Far away from here," she said, and then vanished down the hatch in the floor.

CHAPTER 7

William was lying on top of his duvet with his clothes on, staring at the ceiling. It was 3.30 in the morning and he was still wide awake. He knew he wasn't going to be able to fall asleep. He was thinking about what his mother had said about the accident and how he'd almost died. How had he survived? Did his grandfather's disappearance have anything to do with it? His stomach ached every time he thought about what had happened at the museum. Soon the whole world would know who'd solved the Impossible Puzzle. It was his fault they had to go on the run again.

William heard his parents downstairs in the living room. They were packing up the essentials. The plan was to leave as soon as it was light.

William sat up in bed and looked around at his dark bedroom. Was it suddenly colder in here? He got up and went over to the window, but stopped when he stepped on something hard. There was something on the floor. He squatted down. It was a beetle, lying on its back with its little legs up in the air. William carefully poked it with his finger. It didn't react. He picked it up and put it in his hand.

William carefully set the beetle on top of his desk. He opened one of the drawers and pulled out a magnifying glass so he could examine the little creature. This was no ordinary beetle. It was made up of tiny metal pieces held together by microscopic screws. A mechanical beetle! And one of the most beautiful and most advanced constructions he'd ever seen.

How had it got in? He glanced up at the window and noticed a small hole in the glass pane. The beetle twitched all of a sudden, startling William. He leaped off the chair and stumbled backwards.

The little beetle flipped over and landed on its legs. Then it jumped off the edge of the desk, landing on the floor with a *clack!* It stood watching William for a while before it again gathered speed and scurried around the room. It stopped when it came across a pencil lying under the desk, which it picked up, carried over to William, and set on the floor in front of him. It was acting like a playful dog! William smiled and picked up the pencil.

"Do you want to play?"

The beetle jumped up and down. William tossed the pencil. It hit the wall and landed on the floor. The beetle ran over, picked it up again and delivered it back at William's feet. William grinned, impressed.

"Wow, you're fast," he said. Then he got the pencil again and threw it a little harder.

The pencil hit the doorframe and bounced onto the landing. The beetle darted out, but this time it didn't come back. It picked up the pencil again and stayed out on the landing, peering in at William. "Come," said William.

But the beetle didn't come. It restlessly tapped its leg on the wooden floor, as if it wanted William to follow it out of his bedroom.

"Come here!" William commanded, but the beetle didn't move. He approached it cautiously.

"Stay, staaaay," he said in a calm voice.

He stopped right in front of the beetle and squatted down cautiously. He held out his hand, but before he could grab the beetle, it had darted towards the stairs.

"No, no, no," whispered William, rushing after it.

The beetle paused at the top of the stairs and set down the pencil. William stopped a few metres away.

"Don't go downstairs," William pleaded.

But the beetle kept going. William leaned forward and peered into the dark hallway below. Where had it gone?

He heard his parents talking quietly. William crept further down the stairs and leaned over the banister.

"I don't know," he heard his dad say. "It could be a coincidence, of course, but I don't think we can take any chances."

"Did you talk to the Institute?" his mum asked.

"Yes, they're on their way," his dad replied. "Obviously they already knew about what happened at the museum. I'm quite certain they're the ones behind the whole Impossible Puzzle world tour."

"Trying to track him down?" his mum asked.

"It's in his genes. They knew they just had to wait until he took the bait," his dad said.

"Sending him back to England, though… Isn't there any other option?"

"It's better to get him out of the country for a while. We can't take any chances. The Institute is probably the safest place for him right now."

"I'm so tired of this, tired of hiding. I want my old life back." His mum sounded like she was crying.

"Me too, but we have no choice," his father said.

A sound drew William's attention away from the conversation in the living room. He peered again into the dark hallway. He had lived in this house for most of his life. He knew it well. Especially the sounds it made. The way the walls creaked in a storm. And how the roof crackled on a hot summer's day. But the sound he heard now was a new one. It was a dry clanking sound. Like metal on metal. And it came from the hallway below.

Clank … clank … clank…

William leaned even further over the banister and squinted into the darkness.

Clank … clank … clank…

Suddenly he spotted a large shadow, which moved along the wall and then disappeared. William was about to call out, but he was interrupted by his father, who suddenly screamed at the top of his lungs, "WILLIAM! GET OUT OF THE HOUSE! RUN! RUN!"

William stood on the landing, completely paralysed. He heard his mother wail and then his father shouted again, "RUN, WILLIAM, RUN!"

William turned and ran. He dashed into his bedroom and shut the door behind him. The whole house seemed to be shaking.

Then he heard heavy footsteps on the staircase, which creaked and thumped as the footsteps came closer. They stopped just outside his door.

William stood still, holding his breath, listening. Nothing. Not a sound.

It was completely quiet. Way too quiet.

Then he heard a tapping sound from somewhere in front of him. He looked up, scanning the room with scared eyes. The window!

He darted towards it just before the door was smashed to smithereens behind him. He yanked up the window and flung himself out into the darkness.

CHAPTER 8

William landed heavily in the snow.

He tumbled forwards into a somersault before leaping back onto his feet and running away across the garden, still in only his socks. But there was no time to worry about that, he just had to get away.

Rumbles and crashes could be heard coming from the house behind him. It sounded as if someone was destroying his bedroom.

Seconds later, William was sprinting and sliding across the icy road. He heard a window shatter and something heavy land in the snow. Then the wooden fence exploded into kindling behind him.

Something was after him. Something big.

Clank ... clank ... clank... The sound he had heard in the hallway.

William ran through someone's garden. He wondered if he ought to knock on one of the neighbours' doors, but quickly rejected that idea. He stumbled on, continuing into a street he didn't recognize. His feet were hurting now, his lungs ached and the muscles in his thighs burned. His legs were giving out. He didn't know where he was going, only that he had to keep running. Suddenly the ground fell away beneath him and he tumbled down a slope. He struggled to his feet and looked around, gasping for breath. He was at the edge of a big field. He glanced back. There was no sign of whatever it was that was after him. Had he escaped?

William fought to get his thoughts in order. His body was trembling from the cold, and it had started snowing again. Large flakes wafted down from the dark sky.

William kept moving across the field, but the deep snow made it difficult. He stopped at a tall chain-link fence at the far end of the field and peered through at what lay beyond. It looked like some kind of abandoned industrial estate. He climbed over the fence and headed for one of the dilapidated buildings.

The door was missing. William went inside. Rusty water dripped from the roof. A truck with no wheels sat in one corner. Legs trembling, William headed for the truck and peered inside. He tried the door. It was locked. He looked around and spotted an adjustable wrench on the warehouse floor. He used it to break the truck window and then climbed in.

His body ached and his head felt as if it were about to explode. He just had to make it through the night. He could find help in the morning. His first priority would be to find his parents. Had they made it out? William noticed a shadow move past the door of the warehouse. He sat up and leaned towards the windscreen, peering out into the darkness for several minutes. Nothing. Just snowflakes drifting down. William rested his head back against the seat again.

Suddenly it was as if a bomb had gone off right above him. A large iron beam crashed onto the bonnet of the truck with such force that it shattered the windscreen. William shut his eyes tight and curled up as more beams and sheets of corrugated iron rained down around the truck.

Then everything went quiet again.

William cautiously opened his eyes. The whole roof of the building had been torn off. It was snowing too hard for him to be able to see if there was anything up there.

Something moved over by the door. Two shadowy figures entered the building. One of them was carrying something that looked like a gun, which pulsed with a fierce light. The man raised the gun and pointed it at William, cringing in the cab of the truck.

Suddenly a large iron claw thundered onto the roof, grabbed hold of the truck and yanked it up into the air with tremendous force. William screamed and clung to the steering wheel. The last thing he saw was a blinding ray of light hitting the truck.

Then everything went black.

CHAPTER 9

William was lying on something soft. His body rocked gently back and forth. A faint hum lured him out of sleep. What had just happened? Something about snow ... a bang and a strong light... Then he remembered his father's frightened voice yelling, "RUN, WILLIAM, RUN!" And the little beetle scurrying away, and the truck... William sat up and looked around.

He was in the back seat of a car that was driving fast along a deserted motorway. William put his hands to his head and felt a bandage on his forehead. He checked the rest of his body. Apart from being a little sore, he seemed to be more or less intact.

He leaned forward and peered through the glass divider separating him from the front of the car. Two men with red hair were sitting there. Could they be the people he'd seen in the warehouse? He felt panic rising. Who were they? What did they want with him? Were these the men he and his family had been hiding from for the last eight years?

He made eye contact with one of them in the rearview mirror. The man regarded him with small, cold eyes before looking away again. William tried to relax back into his seat. If they wanted to kill him, he'd already be dead by now, right? Maybe they'd saved him from whatever was after him? Cautiously he knocked on the glass divide. The men didn't respond. He knocked a couple more times, each time a little harder.

"WHO ARE YOU?" he yelled. They didn't turn around.

Suddenly the glass in front of him went dark and then the image of a beautiful woman with rich brown hair and big blue eyes gave him a friendly smile.

"Welcome, William Wenton," she said in a silky voice.

William stared at the image. William *Wenton*? How did she know his real name? William studied the crystal-clear picture. The lady smiled at him with dazzling white teeth.

"My name is Malin, and it's my pleasure to welcome you to the Institute for Post-Human Research," she said. "In a little while, we will be arriving at Gardermoen Airport outside Oslo. From there, our private plane will take you to Heathrow Airport. Then your journey will continue to the Institute, which is idyllically situated in rural England. You will receive more information on the plane. Until then, I wish you a pleasant trip."

"Thanks," mumbled William.

"In the meantime, I have a greeting from your parents," Malin continued. "They're in safe hands."

"In safe hands," William repeated to himself. So his parents were alive. Tears sprang to his eyes. Before he could say anything, his mum and dad appeared on the screen. They were sitting in the back seat of a car that looked just like the one William was in.

"William…" his mother began, struggling against tears. "William, darling. This wasn't how it was supposed to be. I'm just so happy you weren't hurt or…" His mother paused. She swallowed and wiped her eyes with a tissue. "It won't be too long before we're together again."

His mother glanced at his father and took his hand.

"There's so much we should have told you, William. But we thought it was best that you knew as little as possible. They'll explain everything when you arrive at the Institute," his father said with a smile.

"I love you so much, sweetie," his mum said.

"I love you, too," whispered William before the picture flickered a couple of times and disappeared.

William stared at the glass in front of him, as if he expected the image of his parents to reappear. But it didn't. He thought about what they'd said. What was this "Institute"? Should he ask the two men? Surely they were from the Institute, but they didn't really seem like the chatty types. That would have to wait. All William could do was trust that his parents knew what they were talking about, that he was safe and that they were all right too. He leaned back into the soft seat, more relaxed now, and watched the countryside passing by.

A few hours later they pulled into an off-limit area at Gardermoen Airport, where a shiny passenger plane sat waiting for them. A man in a pilot's uniform waved to them before disappearing inside the cockpit. The car stopped right in front of the nose of the plane. Then William heard the sound of electric motors as the front of the plane opened, like the jaw of a gigantic shark. When the jaw was fully open, the car drove on board.

CHAPTER 10

William had the entire aeroplane cabin to himself, and it wasn't just any old aeroplane cabin. Everything around him was shiny and white. There were no seats, just two big white sofas. He was sitting on one of them, buckled in securely. It was like being in some kind of luxury spaceship, William thought.

The plane was already in the air, and down below he could see a layer of clouds. It was quiet in the cabin, the only sound the distant whirr of the engines.

William jumped when the table in front of him suddenly pulled apart and a screen rose up between the two halves. It showed a blue logo that read: *Institute for Post-Human Research*. The logo rotated a couple of times before vanishing, replaced by Malin. She smiled at him, once again showing her dazzling white teeth.

"Welcome aboard, William Wenton. We at the Institute for Post-Human Research warmly welcome you as a new candidate," she said in a pleasant although monotone voice. "We hope you've had a pleasant journey thus far. You will be offered a food and beverage service soon."

"Candidate?" William said.

"One of our information-bots will answer any questions you might have very soon," she continued. "In the meantime, please enjoy a virtual tour of the Institute."

Photos of an enormous white building rolled across the screen in front of him.

"The Institute was founded in 1967 and since then has worked tirelessly on research that will benefit all of humanity," Malin continued.

The building's glossy white exterior was every bit as sleek as the aeroplane William was travelling in.

"Here at the Institute for Post-Human Research, the past and the present merge together in a perfect union. The Institute specializes in researching biotechnology and artificial intelligence," Malin explained. "Every year the Institute admits a group of candidates who have distinguished themselves in the field of codebreaking, cryptography and problem-solving. As a candidate at the Institute for Post-Human Research, you will enjoy the use of all our facilities. We will be at your service to help make your time here as productive as possible. Thank you for your attention."

Then the screen went blank and sank back down into the table.

William sat and wondered what it was he'd just seen. The

Institute for Post-Human Research? Why in the world was he being sent there?

And what was a *candidate*?

William heard a door sliding open at the front of the cabin and spotted a serving trolley heading towards him. The cart stopped with a sudden squeak.

"We can offer you wholewheat or white bread with synthetic ham or synthetic tofu," announced the trolley as a robot arm shot out from the side and pointed at a selection of bottles and baguettes on a tray. If you're thirsty, you can choose between synthetic water, synthetic orange juice and Mars juice."

"Why is everything synthetic?" William asked, leaning forward to get a better look.

"Because that's the way it is," said the trolley impatiently.

William hesitated as his eyes scanned the bottles and plastic-wrapped baguettes. They didn't look synthetic at all.

"So, what'll it be?" said the trolley, wheeling closer.

"Uh, wholewheat with ham and Mars juice," William said, bewildered.

"An excellent choice. The Mars juice is at its best at this time of day," the trolley said as a lid popped up and a robot arm placed the sandwich and a glass of purple juice on the table in front of him.

"Enjoy your meal," the trolley said. "A trash-bot will come and clean up once you've finished."

The trolley squeaked again as it reversed back to the front of the plane at high speed.

"But…?"

"A trash-bot will come to clean up. Take as much time as you need. No hurry," called the trolley and then disappeared through the doorway.

William peered at the food in front of him. He unwrapped the sandwich and smelled it. What in the world was synthetic ham? And Mars juice?

He took a tentative bite and chewed. The ham tasted much like normal ham, only better. He took another bite and another. Soon he was wolfing it down. This had to be the best sandwich he'd ever eaten.

Afterwards he took a sip of the Mars juice, which had changed colour and was now red. It tasted like sweet strawberry and vanilla ice cream. *Weird*, William thought, and took another swig. This time it tasted of oranges, and he realized the juice wasn't red any more. It was orange.

Then the door opened again and the trolley came wheeling towards him. "Trash?" it asked politely.

"Aren't you the same trolley that…?"

"No, I am not!" the offended trolley protested as a mechanical hand shot up and snatched the empty plastic wrapper and napkin. "Thank you. Enjoy the rest of your trip," the trash-bot said, backing away.

"But I was just wondering…"

"An info-bot will answer any questions you have," the trolley said, disappearing through the door.

William settled back, closed his eyes and tried to collect his thoughts. Yet again he heard the sound of the door at the front of the cabin opening. He opened his eyes again. The same trolley was coming back down the centre aisle. It stopped next to him with a jerk.

"Questions?" it asked.

"Yes, are you the serving trolley, the trash-bot *and* the info-bot all in one?" William asked.

"If you have existential questions, you must bring these up with the philosopho-bot! I can send him out next. Was there anything else?"

"Why am I here?" William asked.

The cart said, "Uh…" but then went silent. The little blinking lights went out. It almost seemed as if it had turned itself off. Or short-circuited.

"Hello?" William said cautiously, knocking on the trolley. All he got in response was a hollow, metallic sound. It was like knocking on the side of an empty toaster.

The trolley continued to sit there.

Then suddenly its lights came back on and it hummed to life again. "Apologies for the delay," the trolley said. "Your questions will be answered when you arrive at headquarters."

William slumped back in the seat. He was too tired to argue with a trolley.

"Was there anything else? I do have a great deal of information about air travel, waste management and synthetic food production."

"No thanks. I'm fine," William said.

"Enjoy the rest of your trip. We will be landing in one hour and thirteen minutes," the trolley said, reversing away. "If I were you, I would get some shut-eye," it called before disappearing through the door at the end of the aisle.

William turned his head and looked out of the window. Outside was only darkness. But sleep was the furthest thing from his mind right now. He was tired, but his mind was racing with questions.

Where was he headed? And what had happened to his parents?

CHAPTER 11

William awoke with a start and looked around fearfully.

He was lying on the back seat of the same car as before. The last thing he remembered was getting back into the car and driving off the plane. Then they had travelled through endless roads deep into the English countryside. He must have finally given in to tiredness and dozed off.

The car had come to a stop in front of a large stone staircase. William blinked the sleep out of his eyes and sat up.

He recognized the building from the video on the plane. It looked even bigger in real life. Suddenly there was a knock on the car window and a gloved hand gestured for him to get out. The door slid open and William took a cautious step down. He discovered that someone had put a pair of new shoes on his feet.

"Welcome, William Wenton," said a tall, dark figure, bowing deeply, his face expressionless. He was wearing a black tuxedo with tails, a white shirt and a blue bow tie.

"I'm Tim Cutler," he said in a flat voice, straightening up again.

"William," said William, holding out his hand.

"I know," Cutler said. They shook hands. "I'm the chief butler here at the Institute," he explained. "So … where is it all?"

"Where's what?" William asked.

"Your luggage."

"Oh. I didn't bring anything with me," William said, and smiled apologetically.

Cutler looked at him aghast.

"You don't have anything with you?" he exclaimed. "No clean underwear, socks or anything?"

William shook his head.

"A toothbrush?"

"I left in a bit of a hurry," William said, feeling his cheeks redden.

"All right," the butler said. "This way, please."

William stood and watched as Cutler removed one glove and then waved his hand back and forth in front of a red sensor in the door. The butler lowered his hand and was putting his glove back on when the door emitted two short clicks and swung open.

"After you," he said, gesturing to William.

William walked through, but stopped suddenly when someone yelled, "Watch out!" He looked around but couldn't see where the voice was coming from. Something hit him hard in the legs and he lost his balance and fell over. He sat up, bewildered, and grabbed his shin.

"You need to watch out!" Cutler said from behind him.

"I'm sorry." But William realized that Cutler wasn't scolding him. He was shaking his finger at a small electric vacuum cleaner on the floor in front of him.

"Um, sorry. I was on my way to the TV room. *Terminator* is on," the vacuum cleaner said apologetically, restlessly scooting back and forth.

"Vacuum cleaners don't watch TV," Cutler said. "Back to the docking station with you. You're going to need all the electricity you can get for tomorrow."

"All right." The vacuum cleaner turned around and slowly rolled back the way it had come. "Sorry, man," it mumbled to William as it went by.

"Damn machines," Cutler sniffed, walking on.

William got back up and looked around. They were in a large hall. An enormous chandelier hung from the ceiling. A grand staircase as wide as a four-lane motorway stretched up in front of him, leading to the first floor.

"Are you coming?" Cutler called.

William started to follow, but stopped when he spotted a square metal box with thin little legs coming down the stairs. When the metal box reached the bottom step, it turned around and started climbing back up.

"What is that?" William asked.

"A step-bot," Cutler answered carelessly.

"What does it do?"

"It climbs stairs," Cutler said. "Come on. We don't have all day."

"But what's the point of a robot that can only climb stairs?" William asked, trying to keep up with the butler as he made his way down a long hallway.

"This is a research institution. Most things here are experimental. And often completely impractical."

Cutler stopped beside a tall, flat robot standing motionless by the wall as if it was trying not to be seen.

"Take this one, for example," Cutler continued. "This is the most useless of them all. An argu-bot," he said, his voice filled with disdain.

"Pure lies and malicious rumours," the argu-bot retorted tersely.

"What does an argu-bot do?" William asked.

"It argues, of course," Cutler said, beginning to move off again.

"Well, it beats being a cheap penguin impersonator in a butler's uniform," the argu-bot snapped back.

Cutler froze, then turned back. "What did you just say?"

"Nothing," the argu-bot said. "Just that you're quite fat considering you're so short!"

Cutler walked right up to the argu-bot and growled through clenched teeth, "One of these days, when you least expect it, I'm going to come and pull your plug." He sneered wickedly.

"I run on batteries," the robot said.

"Rubbish," Cutler replied, pointing to a cord that was plugged into a nearby socket. "What's that, then?"

"That's for the lamp," the argu-bot said, nodding at a floor lamp next to him.

"Don't you dare!" the lamp said indignantly.

Cutler shook his head and rolled his eyes.

"You see what I mean by useless?" he muttered to William, dashing down the hallway once more. "Come on!"

William hurried after Cutler, catching him up as they passed a chair where a small, round robot sat dangling its long, thin legs over the edge of the seat.

"I suppose this is a sit-bot, then?" William said jokingly.

"You're a quick learner," Cutler said. "I just call him Humpty Dumpty. Ah, here we are." He stopped in front of a large white door. "You can wait in the library until Mr Goffman arrives."

Cutler waved his hand in front of the door a couple of times. It slid open with an electric *swoosh*.

"In you go," he said. "Oh, and watch out for the librarian. He can be a little … um … unpredictable."

CHAPTER 12

William looked around the room in which he now found himself. The walls and ceiling were made of shiny stainless steel, as was the floor. The sofa in the corner looked as if it had never been used. And everything on the desk in front of him was arranged at right angles. He couldn't see a single book anywhere. Actually, this didn't look like a library at all.

"Mr Goffman is just around the corner," a hoarse voice announced.

William turned but couldn't see anyone. He decided to wait. He remembered the butler's warning about the librarian.

"I said, Mr Goffman is just around the corner!" the voice repeated.

"I heard you … but, um, where are you?"

"Here, obviously," the voice said, irritated.

William heard the hum of an electric motor but still couldn't see anyone.

"Behind you," the voice said.

William swung around and spotted a robot on wheels. It had four long arms and was just as shiny as the library itself. It fit in so well with its surroundings that it was almost completely camouflaged.

"Are you the librarian?"

"Correct," the robot said. "Albert."

"Where are all the—?" William began.

But before he could finish his sentence, one of Albert's long metal arms shot out and pricked William's index finger with a tiny needle.

"OW!" William cried. He held up his finger and saw a small drop of red blood.

"Sorry," Albert said as one of his other arms quickly collected the drop of blood with a pipette.

"What are you *doing*?" William yelled, peering at the robot in disbelief.

"Just a little blood test, completely harmless," Albert said, rolling to the side. "There. In the meantime, have a seat on the sofa. Here's something to read while you're waiting. This is a library after all."

Albert held out an e-reader. William hesitated a moment before taking it and sitting down on the sofa. Then he suddenly felt something yank his hair.

"Ow!" he yelled again, looking at the robot in confusion. Albert was holding a tuft of his hair in one of his hands.

"I'm sorry," Albert said guiltily, quickly hiding the tuft of hair behind its back. "Just a standard hair sample. But I've finished now, I promise. No more tests and that's the truth."

William settled back in the sofa and turned on the e-reader. An overview of the books appeared on the screen. *Alternative Mathematics*, the first one was called. Then there was *Pyramid Theory and Mechanical Origami*. William had to smile. The Institute seemed like a place where he could feel at home.

"Perhaps you've read some of them before," said a deep voice behind him.

William turned to see an unusually tall, thin man wearing a black suit and leaning on a white cane. His hair was coal black. He regarded William with deep, dark eyes.

"Did you have a pleasant trip?" he asked.

"Y-yes," William stammered, getting to his feet.

"Good," the man said. Then he turned to address Albert. "Albert, did you get what you needed?"

The robot held out the pipette and the tuft of William's hair.

"You can leave us now," the man said.

Albert wheeled out into the hallway and the door slid shut behind him. The man waited until the door was closed before walking back over to William and holding out his hand.

"Fritz Goffman," he said. "And it's always better to sit than stand," he continued, gesturing that they should be seated. "You won't know anything about me, but I know quite a lot about you." Goffman eyed William seriously.

"Why am I here?" William blurted out.

"It's a long story, but it's for your own good. You'll learn more as time goes on. For now you'll just have to trust me. Is that all right?" Goffman asked.

William studied the tall, thin man for a good while before nodding. "The video on the plane talked about candidates," he said. "Am I a candidate for something?"

"I know things have been moving pretty fast today. You're mostly here because this is the safest place for you right now. But I also think you would make a good candidate. You'll find out more about that tomorrow," Goffman said with a secretive smile. "The lessons here are quite out of the ordinary," he added.

"And where are my parents?"

"They're doing well and are out of danger at a secret location. But it was a close call this time."

"This time?" William asked.

"Yes. This isn't Abraham Talley's first attempt."

Abraham Talley? William gulped. "Who is Abraham Talley?"

"A very … dangerous … man," Goffman said quietly.

"Is he the reason we had to escape to Norway in the first place?" William asked.

Goffman hesitated before answering. "In a way, yes."

"But why is he after us?"

Goffman leaned in even closer to William. "He's not after *us* at all…" Goffman swallowed. "He's only after you."

William stiffened. "Just me?"

"But he won't get you here, William. The Institute is the absolute safest place you can be right now. Until we manage to track down Tobias."

William's heart skipped a beat. *Tobias?* "Y-you mean my grandfather?" he stammered.

"Yes. Tobias Wenton," Goffman said.

"You knew him?"

"I knew him well," Goffman confirmed. "In fact he was one of the original founders of the Institute."

CHAPTER 13

William jogged along next to Fritz Goffman, who was striding purposefully down the hallway. William was still in shock. He couldn't believe what he had just heard about his grandfather.

"Tobias Wenton was – *is* – one of the best cryptographers in the world," Goffman said. "Do you know what a cryptographer is?"

"Someone who cracks codes," William responded.

"Exactly," Goffman smiled. "The Institute hasn't been the same since he disappeared."

"But—" William began.

"I'm sure you have a lot of questions," Goffman interrupted. "And I'll answer them as best I can. But that will have to wait. It's late and we need some sleep. Your room is in the east wing, up the stairs. I think you'll be comfortable there."

William spotted the argu-bot. He expected it to hurl some comment or other at them, but it didn't. Instead it bowed politely as they went by.

"How long do I have to stay here?" William asked.

"As long as there is a risk that Abraham is trying to find you," Goffman said. "However, I promise you it won't be boring. We've tailored the coursework specially to challenge and develop people like you. You've come to the right place."

"People like me?" William said. "So I *am* a … candidate?"

"We'll see. Since you'll be with us for a while one way or the other, you might as well have something to work on," Goffman said with another sly smile and continued on up the stairs.

The step-bot was on its way down the middle of the staircase, but it stopped and scurried sideways to make room for Goffman and William.

They proceeded down a hallway to one of the big side wings and came to a halt in front of a red door, which opened with a *swoosh*.

"The room may not be large, but it has everything you'll need," Goffman said, showing William in. "You'll have a private lesson first thing tomorrow with Benjamin Slapperton. He'll explain more about what we do here at the Institute. He's a tad eccentric, but he's one of the best cryptographers we have – well, aside from your grandfather. Goodnight." Goffman backed out of the room and the door closed.

The room was sparsely furnished: a neatly made bed with a tartan quilt and pillow, a dresser and a desk in front of a small window. William sat down on the bed. He thought about what Goffman had told him. Had his grandfather really been one of the Institute's founders? What did they actually do here? And how could Goffman be so sure William would be safe?

William got up and went across to the door to make sure it was properly locked. He wiggled the handle.

"The doors are always locked after eleven p.m.," the door suddenly said. William jumped back in alarm.

"Huh?"

He noticed a speaker right above the door handle.

"You're a talking door?"

"This is just an entry-level position," the door said. "In a year or two I'll have a completely different job. I have ambitions."

"Ambitions?" William repeated.

"Yes, ambitions," the door said firmly. "I'm a fabulous cook. I make the best lasagne you've ever tasted. No doubt about it. I'm going to have my own cooking show."

"How can you make lasagne when you don't have any arms?" William asked, taking a step back. After everything he'd seen at the Institute so far, he wouldn't be surprised if the door suddenly shot out a couple of bendy metal arms.

"OK, you caught me. I'm just kidding. I'm a talking door. Had you fooled for a minute there, though," the door said with a hearty laugh.

William laughed too. He realized it felt good, so he laughed again.

"I know I don't have any right to ask this," the door said a moment later, "but I get so curious when new people come to the Institute."

"Ask away," William said.

"Why are they bringing in a new candidate at this time of year?"

"Maybe instead you could explain to me what a candidate is?" William suggested.

"They haven't told you that?" the door said.

"No."

The door paused for a moment. "Oh dear, I seem to have said too much. Again." It sighed.

"Come on. What's a candidate?" William asked.

The door paused again. "OK. Candidates are code-breakers... Or people who are going to become codebreakers, to be more precise. There, I said it. Don't ask me anything else," it said.

"My grandfather was a codebreaker," William said.

"Oh," said the door.

"I think he worked here at the Institute," William continued.

"What was his name?" the door asked.

William hesitated.

"Come on," the door said impatiently. "It takes two to have a conversation. I tell you something, then you tell me something."

William glanced around to make sure he was alone in the

room. Then he leaned towards the door. "Tobias Wenton," he said.

It felt strange to say his grandfather's name out loud. When he was little, after he'd gone to bed he would sometimes whisper it to himself under the covers. But he had never said it out loud before. He looked at the door, waiting for a reaction, but it didn't make a sound.

"Hello? Are you there?" William asked.

No response. William tapped lightly on the little speaker. "Are you there?"

"Tobias Wenton?" the door whispered. "Are you sure?"

"Yes, completely sure," William said. "Have you heard of him?"

"*Have I heard of him?* Tobias Wenton is the best cryptographer we've had here at the Institute. He actually lived in this room for years."

"He did?" William said, surprised.

"Yes, but he was away travelling a lot. I always looked forward to his return. He had so many funny stories. We were good friends. And then suddenly…" The door faltered.

"He disappeared," William volunteered.

"Exactly. And he took with him…" The speaker crackled. "No, now I've said enough," the door said. "You'll have to talk to Mr Goffman if you want to know more."

"Hold on!" William said. "What did he take with him?"

"Talk to Mr Goffman," the door repeated. "Although those

two weren't exactly the best of friends before your grandfather disappeared…" it blurted out before going silent again.

"They weren't? Why not?" Now William really didn't want the conversation to end.

"I've said too much," was all the door would say.

William stood there for a while. Then he knocked cautiously on the door. "Hello?" he said, but the only response was the wind howling outside. William turned and saw snow whipping against the little window.

He walked over and looked out into the darkness. He felt numb. Everything was so unreal. Like a bad dream. Just a few hours ago he had been at home, back in Norway. Together with his parents. And now it was as if he'd suddenly been shot out from a large cannon and landed in this crazy place where he didn't know any of the rules. His mind bubbled over with questions. Like, who was Abraham Talley? And why was Talley after him?

William felt closer to the truth than he had ever been for as long as he could remember. He looked back into the room. His grandfather had founded this place. He had even slept in this room. William finally felt like he had a chance of finding him.

But why had his grandfather left the place he had helped to build?

CHAPTER 14

"Knock, knock…"

William grunted and pulled the duvet over his head.

"KNOCK, KNOCK!"

"Five more minutes, Mum," he mumbled. "Just five minutes!"

"I am *not* your mother," the door said, a little disconcerted.

Suddenly William remembered where he was. The plane trip, the Institute, Fritz Goffman and the talking door. He sat up in bed, squinting with tired eyes into the sunlight shining through the window and bathing the room in golden light.

"Knock, knock," the door said again.

William looked at the clock. "Why are you nagging me like this? Don't you know how early it is?"

"You think I'm just doing this for my own enjoyment? There is actually someone knocking on me. KNOCK, KNOCK, KNOCK!" it called out again.

William swung his feet over the edge of the bed. "Who is it?" he asked the door.

"Who is it? Isn't that why people usually open doors? To find out who's on the other side?" the door said.

William got up and shuffled over the cold floor. He cautiously opened the door, stuck his head out and looked around.

Not a soul.

Did he smell bacon?

"There's no one there," he said.

"Look down, dummy," the door teased.

On the floor was a tray with steaming eggs, bacon, sausages, baked beans, buttered toast and a cup of tea. William bent down and carefully picked up the tray with both hands. He backed into the room, shutting the door with one foot. He set the tray on the desk and sat down.

"Is this synthetic, like on the plane?" he asked, glancing over at the door.

"As synthetic as it comes, but just as good and much healthier," the door replied.

William stuck his fork into a thick slice of bacon and put it in his mouth. Then he tried the beans and eggs. They tasted great. Before he knew it, the plate was empty.

William took a big gulp of the tea. He could feel his energy starting to return.

He'd been so preoccupied with the delicious breakfast that he hadn't noticed the amazing view from the window. William put down the teacup, pushed the breakfast tray aside and climbed up onto the desk. He pressed his nose to the cold glass.

Outside, a snow-covered park stretched as far as he could see. Huge trees that had to be several hundred years old, pruned bushes, statues and fountains. In the middle of the park was a frozen pond surrounded by benches and small gazebos.

William spotted a snow cloud moving behind a line of tall trees. An oval machine on treads came into view and moved across the garden like an enormous vacuum cleaner. A large, trumpet-like hose sucked in snow and then spat it out as dry snow crystals from a pipe on the top. The snow crystals sparkled in the sunlight before vanishing into thin air.

The snow machine passed a man who was bent over rolling a snowball. The man had a red knitted hat on his head and a thick green scarf around his neck. He stopped at a snow castle and added the snowball to the end. Then he took a couple of steps back, put his hands proudly on his hips and admired his creation. A small, square robot with a blue knitted hat popped up behind the snow castle and nodded approvingly. Suddenly blue flames shot out of the man's feet and he lifted off and flew over to the little robot, his hat falling off mid-flight. The sunlight gleamed off a shiny metallic head. He wasn't a man, but another robot! William stared in fascination at the two robots as they continued making snowballs.

When the cloud of snow behind the machine had cleared, William noticed a gigantic conservatory that had to be the size of a football stadium. It lay beyond a line of trees and William could just make out what was inside. Large winged forms were circling beneath great red lamps suspended from the ceiling, casting a strange glow on the shrubs and plants growing below. He tried to open his window to get a better view. But it was frozen shut and wouldn't budge.

"Knock … knock … KNOCK!"

William jumped in surprise and then hopped down off the desk. "Who is it?" he asked.

"KNOCK … KNOCK … KNOCK!" the door cried even more loudly. "Sorry. I'm programmed to adjust my volume to match the knocking on the outside. This must be Harriet. She's always in a hurry and knocks so hard I have a headache for hours afterwards. Open it before she knocks again."

William hurried over to the door and opened it. A small, rosy-cheeked lady in a grey skirt, lavender-coloured blouse and large glasses stood before him. She was every bit as wide as she was tall and was holding a grey folder under her arm. She waved at William as she restlessly shuffled on her high-heeled shoes.

"We're late. Come on!" she said, turning around and quickly walking away down the hall.

"Get going," the door said. "She doesn't wait." William put on his shoes and dashed out into the hall.

"Come on. We don't have all day!" the woman called. She had already reached the end of the hallway, and William had to run to catch her up.

"I'm Harriet, and I'm taking you to your orientation appointment with Benjamin Slapperton. Are you familiar with him?"

William shook his head. "No, I've just heard his name."

"He's a little odd," Harriet said, giving William a look over the top of her glasses. "But come on, now. We don't have much time."

They rounded a corner and continued down a narrow stone staircase. Harriet's short legs moved like drumsticks, and William had trouble keeping up.

At the bottom of the stairs, Harriet opened a heavy oak door and they emerged from the back of the building. The morning sun shone from a cloudless sky and the sounds of chirping birds could be heard. Without slowing her pace, Harriet sped across the snow-covered park that William had seen from his room. William glanced down at her high-heeled shoes, trudging along on the slippery footpath. He didn't understand how she managed not to fall.

Then he saw the mysterious conservatory. It towered over them like a mountain. Above a set of double wrought-iron doors hung a large sign that said:

CYBERNETIC GARDEN
Do not feed the plants! (Level 3)

"What is that?" William asked.

Harriet glanced at him. "You'll find out soon enough."

"But what does 'Level Three' mean?" he continued.

"That means it'll be a while before they let you in there," she said, speeding up further. "You can be glad about that. It's a dreadful place."

William thought about the sign as they hurried on. He knew what "cybernetic" meant from his grandfather's books. It was the science of advanced technical systems. Something you used when you built robots, for example. William looked over at the plants in the enormous conservatory. If a garden was cybernetic, that meant that it must somehow be synthetic.

William yearned to take a closer look, but that would have to wait. At the moment it was all he could do to keep up with the power walker ahead of him.

"Come on. We don't have all day," Harriet said, jogging over the snow. William hurried after her, but stopped when a snowball suddenly hit her on the back of the head. She howled and spun around.

"What are you doing?" she yelled, glaring at William as she brushed the snow off her neck.

"It wasn't me," William said, scared.

"Nonsense, of course it was y—" she began, but was interrupted by a second snowball, which hit her square in the face, knocking her big glasses off her nose and into the snow.

William turned in the direction the snowball had come

from and spotted the two robots a little way off, standing behind the wall of their snow castle.

"Someday I'm going to have you lot sent to the scrapheap!" Harriet shouted, blowing snow off her glasses.

They didn't seem to care very much about her threats. The larger of the two robots began to make a fresh snowball.

"Hurry up!" Harriet yelled at William. "We're late."

CHAPTER 15

Harriet and William came to a stop outside a stone building with a domed copper roof. This structure looked much older than the main building. A sign saying *Orbatorium* in gilt letters hung over the door, which flew open just at that moment. A man in a white coat poked his head out distractedly. His hair was dishevelled.

"Good morning, Benjamin. I've brought William Wenton for Orientation," Harriet said, nodding in William's direction.

Benjamin Slapperton held his hands up to shield his eyes from the bright sun. He stood squinting at William for a moment.

Finally he said, "William Wenton?" and leaned forward, grabbing hold of William's jumper and tugging him through the doorway. The door slammed shut again in Harriet's face. William could hear her outside, complaining.

"Irritating woman," Slapperton said, looking at William. "Don't you think?"

William squirmed. "I've only just met her."

"Yes, that's right. You'll have to wait to get to know her before you start disliking her," Slapperton said, gesturing towards a chair in front of a large blackboard. "Have a seat."

William sat down and looked about him. The room was round with a high-domed ceiling. The walls were lined with tall shelves filled with mechanical devices of various shapes and designs. A large brass steam engine stood in one corner, and a mechanical eagle hung from the ceiling. William quivered with excitement. Deep inside he knew this was more than just machinery. This room was full of mechanical codes, the kinds of codes he'd read about in his grandfather's books. Codes he'd never thought he would get to see in real life.

"You look like a completely normal boy," Slapperton said, sizing up his new student. "Imagine a boy who looks so ordinary being able to solve something as extraordinary as the Impossible Puzzle!"

Slapperton scratched his dark moustache, which suddenly hopped down onto his shoulder.

"No, come back!" Slapperton yelled, trying in vain to catch the moustache as it moved down his jacket, hopped over onto the desk and continued to zigzag through all the clutter there.

Slapperton upended an empty coffee cup, which he slammed down to capture the rogue moustache.

"Gotcha!" he yelled, then held the squirming moustache

up for William to see. "What do you think?" he asked. "I made it myself."

William hesitated. "What is it?"

"A mechanical moustache. It runs little errands and such for me. Practical as long as it's behaving, but it can get a touch cantankerous at times."

Slapperton put the moustache back on his upper lip.

"But what did I do with … hm…? I mean, I just had it…" Slapperton rummaged around on his desk. "I put it right here. Ah, there it is," he said, picking up something that William immediately recognized. "You've seen this before," Slapperton said, holding out a cylinder. It was the Impossible Puzzle.

"Yes." William blushed. "How did you get it?"

"I made it." Slapperton smiled proudly.

William sat up in the chair. "But…" he began. Dozens of thoughts flooded into his head. "Were you the ones who arranged the museum exhibition?"

"Ah, that… Yes," Slapperton said.

"But why?"

"To find you, of course," Slapperton said, looking at the metal cylinder. "We didn't know where in the world you were. So we sent the device out on a global tour. You inherited a lot from your grandfather and I knew you wouldn't be able to keep yourself away. It took longer to find you than I thought it would. Norway, huh? Who'd have thought? But in the end you took the bait."

William was beginning to feel nervous. If his grandfather hadn't wanted the Institute to find them, maybe it wasn't such a good thing that he was here.

"I know what you're thinking," Slapperton said. "Why didn't your grandfather want us to find you."

William looked up at him and nodded.

"Tobias had become a tad paranoid before he disappeared, especially after your accident. He didn't want to take any chances, and sent your family away to Norway."

"But why did you want me?" William asked.

"Mostly because we think you're safer here," Slapperton said. Then, clearing his throat, he added, "And because I think you can help us find him."

"My grandfather?" William exclaimed.

"Yes," Slapperton said, setting the Impossible Puzzle down.

He pulled something out of his jacket pocket and held it out so William could see. It was a metal sphere the size of an apple and covered with strange symbols.

"All of the candidates get one," Slapperton said, handing the sphere to William. It was cold and heavy. Much heavier than it looked.

There it was again: the *candidates*. William gave Slapperton a questioning look.

"I'm sorry. I forget that you don't know much about the Institute yet," Slapperton said. "The candidates are the next generation of codebreakers – cryptographers in training. They all have special abilities that we're trying to develop here at the Institute. We found them almost the same way we found you – just not under such dramatic circumstances, of course."

"You mean the other candidates won competitions too?" William asked.

"Yes. We have six other candidates here at the moment. The number varies, but it is never that high. We're talking about extraordinarily talented people. And there aren't that many of those. You'll meet them tomorrow. Today you should spend your time familiarizing yourself with your orb."

Slapperton pointed at the sphere sitting in William's hand.

"My orb? Is this an— Ow!"

William caught a brief glimpse of the tiny needle that had just pricked him before it retracted back into the sphere.

"Nothing to worry about," Slapperton said. "It's just making sure you're the right person."

"The right person?" William repeated.

"Each orb is person-specific. I'm sure you remember the samples that were taken when you arrived?"

William nodded.

"This orb has been specially programmed for you. It knows your genetic code, and you're the only one who can use it. And don't worry, it won't prick you every time you pick it up," Slapperton said, smiling wryly. "When you solve it to the first level it will do a full scan of you so that it can recognize you on sight in future."

"On sight?" William repeated.

"Yes. On sight. An orb is a key, but not just any old key. It is a mechanical puzzle that has ten levels. As you solve the levels, the orb will take on new properties. And you will also gain access to new parts of the Institute," Slapperton said. "That's why it's imperative that only the owner can use his or her orb."

William remembered what it had said on the cybernetic garden sign.

"So I have to get to Level Three before I can enter that enormous conservatory out there?" he asked.

"Correct. But you'll have to be patient. It usually takes a couple of weeks to solve the first level."

William glanced down at his orb. It had different parts that could be turned and twisted, just like the Impossible Puzzle. A glowing blue zero blinked on a little display.

"Does this mean I'm a candidate?" William asked.

"Would you like to be one?"

William had to smile. This was almost too good to be true. "Yes," he said.

"Wonderful!" Slapperton clapped his hands. "But I have to go," he added, looking at the time. "You can sit here and familiarize yourself with your orb. You'll find the way back on your own." Slapperton gathered up a stack of papers. "Just shut the door behind you when you leave. If you close it all the way, it will lock automatically," he called, dashing out.

William remained sitting in the chair. He closed his eyes

and cautiously clasped his hands around the orb. He felt the familiar stirring in his stomach right away. A feeling of warmth spread up his spine and out to his arms. It was just him and the orb now. He opened his eyes again.

The symbols had begun to glow, as if they had come free from the orb, and were hovering in the air above it. Some of the symbols became smaller, while others grew and glowed more brightly in different colours. And from nowhere, William detected a pattern. His fingers began twisting and turning the small pieces that held the orb together.

Then it started to vibrate.

The vibrations increased until William was sure it would fall apart in his hands. He let go of the orb and gasped when it didn't fall but remained hovering in the air in front of him. William stared at the metal sphere. The vibrations stopped and something inside the orb clicked twice. It twisted by itself as if it were looking around. Then a blue light shot out of a small hole in the metal. The beam of light hit William, visible as a glowing blue dot in the middle of his forehead, then started darting back and forth at lightning speed. Was it scanning him?

The light travelled sideways up and down his body faster and faster and then began to take on a form. William took a step back and gasped when he saw an image of himself standing in front of him. It was as if the blue laser had made a hologram copy of him.

Then the hologram shrank and disappeared back into the orb, along with the light, as quickly as it had appeared. The orb emitted a couple of electronic beeps, then flew towards William at speed. Stopping at just the right moment, it remained floating in front of him, as if waiting for something. When William, unsure what to do, made no response, the orb moved even closer – poking him a couple of times in the chest – then retreated again.

"You want me to hold you?" William whispered.

William reached out and held his hand under the orb, which fell and landed perfectly in his palm. Cradling it, he noticed the little display had changed from zero to a glowing number one.

William smiled. He had reached the first level. He turned the orb round in his hand and wondered if he could solve two more to get into the cybernetic garden.

He was dying to have a look.

CHAPTER 16

An hour later William still held the orb in his hand. A three was now blinking in the little display. Getting to the next two levels had been progressively more difficult. At Level Two the orb had grown to the size of a beach ball. And when William made it to Level Three, it had shrunk to the size of a marble. But he'd done it and now he was standing in front of the doors to the cybernetic garden.

William put his hand on the cold iron and tried to pull the door open, but it was locked. "I suppose this is where you come in," he said, holding up the little orb.

But what was he actually supposed to do? He remembered what Slapperton had said: the orb worked like a key. He looked the door over. If the orb was a key, there had to be a keyhole somewhere, didn't there?

His eyes came to rest on a round hollow in the door. He peered inside, and discovered engraved there the image of a tiny orb and the number three.

William raised his orb and held it in front of the hollow. Nothing happened.

He moved it a little nearer. Suddenly the orb shot out of his hand, hitting the hollow with a loud bang.

Then it began to spin, and before William knew it the door was sliding open.

"Welcome to the Institute's cybernetic garden," a monotone voice said. "For security reasons, please remain on the marked paths and remember: do not feed the plants. Have a pleasant visit."

"Thanks," William said, putting his orb in his pocket.

The garden was enormous, tall palms and lush trees stretching for as far as he could see. He looked up. It must be a hundred metres to the top, at least. Large birds circled overhead. It was like being in a jungle: hot, overpowering and a little creepy.

A stone path led into the trees ahead. William began to follow it. After passing a small grove of trees, he emerged into what looked like a park with large cages lining the path. William stopped in front of one of the cages and studied the green plant inside. It looked like a completely normal cactus. A little brass plate said *Ferreus ictus*.

"*Ferreus ictus…*" William said to himself, leaning closer. He knew that *ferreus* was Latin for iron and that *ictus* meant bite: iron bite. *Weird name for a cactus,* he thought. And then it occurred to him that surely someone must have given the cactus that name for a reason. William backed away just as the cactus lunged forward, gaping to reveal a large mouthful of sharp steel teeth.

"Wow!" he exclaimed, delighted. He stood and watched the cactus attacking its cage as if it was prey. Then it let go and hissed at William.

"A cybernetic robot cactus," he said to himself. "Cool."

William turned to look at the other cages. There was no doubt about it: almost all the plants looked a little odd. Some of them even had blinking lights here and there. William moved deeper into the garden, reading the names of the plants as he walked by: *Toxicum vegetabilis*, *Pulchra inferna*, *Planta homicida*, *Diabolum infernum*.

He paused by an enormous vine draped between two trees. It looked like a huge green spiderweb. The plant was moving slowly back and forth as if it was swaying in the wind. But there wasn't any wind. William checked the sign: *Viridis polypus*.

"Green octopus," he translated.

He took a couple of steps back and stared at the plant as if he expected something to happen. Suddenly he heard a deafening scream overhead and saw a gigantic bird diving towards him.

William was just about to throw himself to the ground when the vine shot into the air and grabbed the huge bird, wrapping it up in ten thick tendrils. The bird screamed and flapped its enormous wings, but it was stuck tight. Stumbling backwards, William didn't take his eyes off the bird, which was struggling in vain against the greedy plant. The green octopus plant stuffed the desperate creature into its dark cavernous maw. After it had chewed and swallowed, the plant emitted a loud burp, belching out feathers and metallic bone shards and spitting them on the ground.

William realized it was time to get out of there.

He looked around for an exit. He had been so preoccupied with all the plants that he had completely forgotten to keep track of which way he had come. He took his best guess and began to walk. Now all the plants seemed to be reaching for him with hungry, metallic jaws full of razor-sharp teeth.

He sped up.

A tall sunflower turned towards him and growled. William jumped aside and stumbled into a low fence that separated the path from a vast lawn. A sign said *KEEP OFF THE GRASS!* in black letters, but on the far side of the grassy area he could see the wrought-iron doors through which he had come. He hopped over the fence and started running.

It took a few moments before William realized he wasn't moving forwards. He ran faster, but still made no progress. William looked down and saw that the grass was moving backwards beneath him. Every single blade of grass was moving in the opposite direction to the way he wanted to go.

William stopped.

He was starting to panic now. This wasn't normal grass.

He turned around and began cautiously walking back towards the fence again. But the grass just moved in the other direction so that he stayed put, stuck in the same spot. William looked around helplessly.

Without warning, his feet slid from underneath him, knocking the wind out of him as he hit the ground. He lay gasping for breath before trying to get up again, but no matter how hard he struggled, his arms and legs slipped out to the sides.

Then the grass started moving all in one direction. It was as if he was being carried away by thousands of tiny ants. Suddenly he noticed a hole opening up in the middle of the lawn, edged by vicious steel teeth. The hole gurgled and sloshed and a terrible stench rose out of the darkness.

"HELP!" William screamed at the top of his lungs.

He stared in horror as he was drawn nearer and nearer to the gaping mouth. He closed his eyes and put his hands over his face. He was only seconds away from the steel teeth…

The grass stopped moving.

Am I dead? William thought. He didn't dare open his eyes. He lay waiting for the grass to start moving again.

"If you wanted it switched off, you only had to ask!" a voice called out.

William opened his eyes now. He was right beside the gaping hole. His trouser leg had snagged on one of the metal teeth. The fabric ripped as he pulled his leg away. William stood up shakily and saw that someone was standing on the path on the far side of the fence.

It was a girl. She had dark hair pulled into a long plait that hung over one shoulder. She was holding a stack of books in her hands.

"All of the machines have off buttons. Look for it next time you're about to be eaten," she said seriously, pointing to a big red button on a control panel that said *ON/OFF*.

William ventured a smile. "Thank you."

She turned and started to walk away.

"Wait!" William called, running after her.

The girl stopped and cocked her head at him.

William hopped over the low fence, but caught his foot and almost fell. With a couple of unsteady steps he managed to regain his balance.

"Thank you for…" he began, glancing back at the gaping hole in the lawn.

"*Cibi tritor*," she said wryly.

William gave her a questioning look.

"That means meat grinder. Not particularly original, if you ask me. But of course originality is something most of these silly machines lack," she said, looking with disdain at the plants surrounding them.

"What's your name?" he asked.

"Iscia," she told him.

"Like the island off Naples in Italy?" William asked.

She nodded. "But without the *h*."

"Why were you named after an island?" William continued. There was something about this girl that made him curious.

She glanced quickly at the ground. "My parents were married there," she said, looking back up at him.

"Cool," he said. He had a lot more questions but decided to hold back.

"What *is* all this?" he asked, indicating the conservatory around them.

"Experiments, of course. Like the rest of the robots and gadgets the Institute is stuffed with," she said.

"I get the sense that you're not that fond of robots," William said. "Are you one of the candidates?"

"You ask a lot of questions," Iscia said. "How did you get in here anyway?"

"With this," William said and pulled the orb out of his pocket.

"With *that*?" she exclaimed.

"Yes," William said.

"When did you get it?"

"Today."

"You haven't solved your way to Level Three already!"

William blushed and looked down.

"Well, anyway, you don't have any reason to be here. I'm usually the only one who comes inside," Iscia snapped.

She turned and walked away with determined steps. William stood watching her until she disappeared behind two snarling rosebushes.

CHAPTER 17

The next morning, William hopped out of bed and shuffled across the cold floor. He opened the door expecting to find a delicious breakfast as he had the day before but was disappointed when all that was waiting there was a brown paper parcel.

"What are you waiting for?" the door asked. "Open it. This is a big day."

William picked up the package and was even more disappointed to feel that it was soft. He crossed over to the bed and sat down. A handwritten card had been stuck under the tight twine. He pulled out the card and read: "Come to the dining hall at seven a.m. sharp."

William suddenly felt excited. Finally he would get to meet the other candidates. And see Iscia again. He tore open the package and looked at the contents.

A pile of clothes.

He stood up and laid the items out on the bed: a grey

tweed jacket, a light green shirt, a purple tie, a pair of dark blue trousers and a pair of black shoes.

A few minutes later he was standing in front of the mirror looking at himself. The jacket was a bit big. And the trousers were maybe a bit long.

He looked different. Too neat.

William messed up his hair. It didn't help.

He opened the top button of the shirt and loosened the tie a fraction. No better.

His eye fell on a leather patch stitched onto the outside of the chest pocket of the jacket. He moved closer to the mirror. It was a picture of an orb. He took his orb from the bedside table and slid it into the pocket. It fitted perfectly.

"Good luck, William," the door said as he left the room.

As William headed towards the stairs, something made him stop and turn around. An old woman stood at the end of the hall beside a cleaning trolley. She looked at him without acknowledging him. A hummingbird sat on her shoulder. William nodded to her before turning and continuing on his way. He cast one last look back before starting down the stairs, but the old woman was gone.

William paused in the doorway of the big dining hall. There had to be more than a hundred people in there. Mostly grown-ups. A few in white lab coats, others in suits. Various robots scurried back and forth between the round tables. They were serving and clearing at a tremendous pace.

"William Wenton?" a voice asked.

William turned and saw a tall, thin robot in a black suit rolling towards him on four wheels.

"Yes," he replied.

"Follow me," the robot said and headed into the hall.

William followed, weaving between the tables. Some of the adults glanced up from their food and nodded. William nodded back. But most of them were too busy eating to notice him.

"William," he heard someone say behind him.

He spun around and saw Slapperton sitting alone at a table.

Slapperton waved. "You'll be seeing me after breakfast. We'll talk then," he said with a smile.

William nodded briefly and continued to follow the wait-bot.

"Here you go. You will sit here." The robot pointed with a thin arm at a table where Iscia was sitting with three boys and two other girls. Six pairs of eyes looked up from their plates to stare at William.

They were wearing the same uniform as him and looked about his age. William didn't think they looked particularly brainy… In fact, they seemed completely normal. They could've been in his class back home in Norway.

As he sat down, Iscia acknowledged him briefly then carried on eating.

Was she angry because of what had happened yesterday?

Because he was at the same level as her? Or because he'd intruded on her turf? William shook his head. He had enough to worry about – she could have the garden to herself for all he cared.

CHAPTER 18

"Just my luck," Slapperton moaned. "It won't budge."

He was standing on a stepladder using his pointer to thwack one of the rolled-up projector screens that hung over the whiteboard.

Each of the students – or candidates, as William now knew them to be – was already in his or her own seat, watching Slapperton impatiently. The teacher straightened up on the stepladder, wobbling precariously. Then he tugged hard on the screen handle, which suddenly came unstuck. The ladder tipped and Slapperton fell backwards, unravelling the chart as he went and landing on his back on the desk. He leaped up, beaming triumphantly.

"You see? Anything is possible as long as you don't give up!" he exclaimed, hopping down off the desk.

"Today is a bit of a special day, gang. We have a new candidate on the team. Let's welcome William Wenton." Slapperton pointed to William and smiled. "He's joining us all the way from Norway."

"Norway?" one of the other boys called out. Someone laughed.

"Do you have your orb with you?" Slapperton continued, ignoring the others.

William nodded.

"Did you get anywhere with it yesterday?"

William hesitated. He glanced at the other candidates and said nothing.

"I understand," Slapperton said. "Most people find the first level the most difficult."

William nodded vaguely.

"He's on Level Three," someone announced drily from the back of the room. William peered over his shoulder. It was Iscia.

A gasp went through the small group. Slapperton broke out into a violent coughing fit.

"Level Three?" he asked, clearing his throat. "Let me see that!"

William pulled the orb from his chest pocket and held it out. Slapperton snatched it from him, then strode back to his desk. He mumbled to himself as he twisted and turned the orb, scratching his head, his back to the class. After he'd stood like that for what seemed like for ever, he turned and peered at William through narrowed eyes. William was sure there were going to be consequences. That he had broken some rule or other and that they were going to take the orb away from him, or kick him out of the group.

"How did you manage to…?" Slapperton pointed to the number three in the display.

William didn't respond.

Slapperton scanned the rest of the group.

"How many of you have reached Level Three?" he asked, holding up William's orb.

No one answered.

"How many?" he asked again. Iscia raised her hand.

"No one else?" Slapperton asked. "Freddy?" Slapperton pointed to a tall boy with curly brown hair. Freddy shook his head and gave William a dirty look.

"This is most extraordinary, William," Slapperton said, returning the orb to him.

William quickly put it back in his pocket.

"We have had many gifted candidates here at the Institute. But this…" Slapperton continued, pulling a white remote control out of his pocket. He stood staring at William for a moment before he shook off his surprise and decided to proceed.

"The history of technology, that's what we'll be learning more about today. How far did we get?"

William glanced around at the others. Freddy glared back at him. "Ancient Egyptian batteries," Iscia said.

"Ah, yes, ancient Egyptian batteries. And lamps that ran off electricity four and a half thousand years ago," Slapperton said, aiming the remote at the screen.

"This is what they looked like," he continued as an image

of a clay vase appeared. "They were constructed the same way as modern batteries. Very simple, actually."

Slapperton pressed the remote control again. The clay vase disappeared, replaced by a basket of potatoes.

"How many potatoes does it take to light up a light bulb?" he asked, looking out at the small class. "And, no, this isn't one of those how-many-people-does-it-take light bulb jokes," he added with a smile.

Iscia raised her hand.

"Anyone else?" Slapperton asked.

"One," William said.

Iscia gave him a dirty look.

"Yup. There's enough electricity in one potato to power a light bulb," Slapperton said.

William had seen potato lamps like that before, in one of his grandfather's books. Slapperton stuck the remote control back into his pocket and moved around behind his desk. He picked up two boxes. One was full of potatoes and the other contained light bulbs and wires.

"Now let's see if it works," Slapperton said and looked at the small group of students. "Get up here and take whatever you think you need to get the light bulbs going."

There was a quick rustle and scraping of chairs as the students stood up and headed towards the front of the class. William was the last in line, but he returned to his desk with a potato, a couple of copper leads and a small light bulb.

He put the potato on his desk and looked at the others, who were already experimenting. No one had managed to light their bulbs yet. William knew that all he had to do was divide the potato into a positive and a negative section, insert the copper wires and connect them to the light bulb. Pretty simple actually. As long as you knew the principle.

A minute or two later, William leaned back and surveyed the white light coming from the little LED bulb.

"Wonderful, William," he heard Slapperton say. "Since you've finished, maybe you could help the others."

William felt himself blushing. He had no desire to show the others anything at all. He looked around. A couple of the candidates glared at him. *Typical*, thought William. *They already don't like me.*

"Hold on one second, William," Slapperton called when the class was over and everyone was on the way out. "Could you stay behind for just a moment?"

William stopped in his tracks, and Freddy bumped into him from behind.

"Sorry," William said.

"Idiot," Freddy muttered.

"Close the door and come over here for a sec," Slapperton said. He followed William with his eyes, as if he wanted to tell him something. As if he was considering whether or not he should.

"I knew your grandfather very well," he said finally.

William waited for him to go on.

"We were good friends right up until he disappeared. We went on digs all over the world together. Maybe I shouldn't tell you this…" Slapperton hesitated.

"Tell me what?"

Slapperton leaned closer and whispered, "Have you ever heard of luridium?"

CHAPTER 19

Professor Slapperton walked over to a shelf full of test tubes. He put his index finger in one of the tubes and pushed it down a couple of centimetres. Then he did the same with some of the others and took a step back. There was a restrained clinking as the shelf suddenly swung aside, revealing a dark passageway behind.

"Come. There's something I want to show you," Slapperton said, disappearing into the darkness.

The ceiling was just high enough for Slapperton to walk upright.

"Where are we going?" William asked, following the professor into the passageway.

Slapperton pulled a small torch out of his jacket pocket and turned it on.

"Down here," he said, heading down a couple of narrow steps at the end of the passage. It smelled like old mould, and the walls were slippery with green algae. "The Institute is built on the foundations of an old castle," he explained.

William shuddered. Dark, narrow passageways were not his thing. But if this would help him find out more about his grandfather, he would just have to steel himself and get on with it.

"We're almost there now," Slapperton whispered, stopping in front of an ancient door.

The door gave a deep rumble as it swung open. Slapperton turned and gave William a serious look.

"You must promise not to tell anyone about what you see in here. This is one of the best-kept secrets at the Institute."

William nodded.

Slapperton turned back and went in. William hesitated.

"I can't switch on the light until you're in and we've closed the door," Slapperton said.

William stepped into the darkness. The heavy door banged shut behind him and he jumped. He stood waiting, fear washing over him. Then he heard a soft *click*, and a light flickered on the ceiling. William looked around him at the small brick room in which he now found himself. Slapperton was standing next to something that looked like an old control panel. Otherwise the room was empty. Slapperton waved him over.

William had a sinking feeling in the pit of his stomach. He was in a secret cellar beneath the Institute's foundations with a man he didn't know. And no one else knew he was here.

"You said you were going to show me something. What

does this have to do with my grandfather?" William's voice sounded unsteady.

"Turn away for a moment," Slapperton said.

As he did so, William heard the squeak of old metal buttons being pressed. Then Slapperton came and stood next to William. The floor beneath them started booming.

"Now you can look!" Slapperton whispered, pointing to the floor in the centre of the room.

A round column slowly rose up out of a hole in the floor that was about the size of a manhole cover. It stopped when it was as tall as Slapperton.

"Amazing, eh?" Slapperton said, moving towards it. William followed.

An opening appeared in the side of the stone cylinder, revealing thick glass behind it.

"This is completely burglar-proof and has been kept under the highest security. Even so, what used to be in there is gone now," Slapperton said.

A faint blue light, almost like a ghostly mist, pulsed behind the glass. William stood entranced.

"What is it?" he asked.

But Slapperton didn't answer. He, too, was staring at the light flickering behind the thick glass.

"Professor Slapperton?" William asked uncertainly. Slapperton snapped out of his trance.

"Luridium," he said. "Or ... well, to be completely accurate

… it *was* luridium. It's gone now. The light is the only thing left to prove it was there."

"Like radiation?" William asked.

"In a way," Slapperton said.

He gestured for William to take a closer look. William peered at the container behind the glass. It was true: the column was completely empty.

"What's luridium?" he asked.

"Luridium is a kind of metal." Slapperton cleared his throat. "Or, to be precise, intelligent metal. In other words, a metal that can think for itself."

"Intelligent metal?" William repeated.

"It's composed of minuscule computers the size of atoms and can be programmed to take any form. Even a human brain. It's like a smart, liquid computer program," Slapperton said. A sombre look came over his face. "Luridium is the most dangerous and most fascinating technology in the world. If it ends up in the wrong hands…" Slapperton paused. His eyes took on a vacant look. "But that's not the most amazing thing," he added.

"What is, then?" William asked.

"Luridium is very old and had been buried under thick layers of stone and coal for millions of years until a lump was discovered at the beginning of the 1860s."

William glanced up at Slapperton. "What happened?"

"It was when work began on digging the tunnels for the

109

underground trains in London. One of the miners, a man named Abraham Talley, happened upon a lump of luridium while he was working on the first tunnel."

Abraham Talley, William thought. Goffman had mentioned him. The man who was after William.

"A terrible accident occurred right after the luridium was found," Slapperton said. "Ten workers were killed. And Abraham was the only survivor. He was taken to hospital, where he spent three days in a coma. By the time they figured out how the other workers had died, it was too late. Abraham had disappeared from the hospital without a trace."

"What do you mean? How had they died?" William asked.

"They were strangled. By Abraham." Slapperton hesitated, studying William as if to check this wasn't too much for him.

"But why?" William asked.

"To cover up what he'd found. The luridium had already taken over his body. It was taking over his mind, too."

A thought struck William. "But … if Abraham Talley discovered luridium over a hundred and fifty years ago, that would mean that…"

"He's very old, yes," Slapperton continued. "That's a side effect of having luridium in your body. Abraham vanished without a trace until he turned up again a hundred years later, in 1960. That was when your grandfather and a couple of colleagues founded the Institute, to keep the luridium from falling into the wrong hands. They began searching for other sources of luridium too, and hid what little they found here at the Institute, in this room, to keep Abraham from getting hold of it."

"Abraham? But why did he come back?"

"To get more. He needed a refill," Slapperton said.

"Where is he now?" William asked.

"We don't know. He disappeared again eight years ago. Around the same time as your grandfather."

"Was he the one who attacked my family back home in Norway?" William was trembling now.

"I don't think so. Probably one of his helpers," Slapperton said.

"But then Abraham managed to steal the luridium from the Institute anyway?" William pointed to the empty container.

"Someone stole it, yes – but it wasn't Abraham," Slapperton said.

"Who was it, then?" William asked.

"Your grandfather."

CHAPTER 20

By the time William finally reached the dining hall the next morning, the others had almost finished eating. He took a plate and helped himself to breakfast from the buffet. He nodded at the other candidates before sitting down in his spot and wolfing down his food. He was starving.

His mind had been in a whirl after everything Slapperton had told him yesterday: the luridium, Abraham Talley, his grandfather. Especially the part about his grandfather. William had hardly slept as a result, and his head felt as if it were filled with syrup.

He needed to try to think about something else.

Iscia was sitting across from him, poking at her food with her fork. He tried to catch her eye, but she was staring fixedly at her plate.

"Let me see your orb," a hoarse voice hissed from the other end of the table.

William looked up and saw Freddy, chewing with his

mouth open, fix him with a glare. William took a bite of boiled egg and didn't respond. He didn't want any trouble.

But Freddy wasn't about to back down.

"No newbie gets to Level Three on his orb in just one day, not without cheating."

William tried to ignore him. He focused on his food and slumped in his chair in an effort to make himself seem smaller. But this tactic didn't seem to have any effect on Freddy. He loaded his fork and pulled back on it, aiming at William. A piece of bacon hit William right on the forehead and flopped down into his lap.

"Leave him alone," Iscia snapped, without looking up.

"Shut up," Freddy said gruffly.

"I just want to eat in peace," Iscia said.

"I said, shut up," Freddy said.

With a loud splat, half an egg hit her on the temple and fell onto her plate. Iscia clenched her fists and closed her eyes. William looked over at Freddy, who had a piece of sausage on his fork now and was taking aim at him a second time.

William lowered his gaze and carried on eating.

"I suppose you think you're better than us just because you had beginner's luck with your orb?" Freddy hissed.

"Keep it down over there!" one of the teachers called.

William's forehead broke into a cold sweat and adrenaline coursed through his veins. They sat eating in silence for a while longer. William was just beginning to think he could relax again, when suddenly the piece of sausage hit him square on the nose.

"Just ignore him," Iscia whispered. "He has the concentration of a goldfish, he's bound to give up soon."

William looked up and met Iscia's eyes. He felt a new strength growing within him.

"I said *shut up!*" Freddy was really angry now. A clump of scrambled egg hit Iscia right on the eye. "No one here is interested in what you have to say," he hissed, reloading his fork.

"Cut it out," William said.

"Oh, hey, he *can* talk!" Freddy said snidely. William and Freddy stared at each other for a moment.

"OK, two o'clock behind the Orbatorium. You're dead!" Freddy barked, then he stood up and marched out.

CHAPTER 21

It was two o'clock and William was standing behind the Orbatorium.

They didn't seem to clear the snow back here very often, it came all the way up to his knees. But he was far too tense to even notice the cold. He didn't usually end up in situations like this. Maybe it was because he hadn't slept well. Or because of what Slapperton had told him. He looked around nervously. Perhaps Freddy had got cold feet? Or had forgotten about the whole thing. William decided to wait a couple more minutes. At least he could say that he had showed up. His fingers ached from the cold. He cupped his hands over his mouth and blew into them. It didn't help. They still trembled.

"Look at him!" He suddenly heard Freddy's hoarse voice. "Like a scared little bunny in the snow."

William turned and saw Freddy and two of the other boys standing a short distance away.

"I'm ready," William blurted out. It was a lie, but what else could he say?

"You don't look ready," Freddy sneered. "You've never even been in an orb duel before, have you?" He snickered, holding up his orb.

An orb duel? William was confused. What was Freddy talking about? William had thought this was going to be a good, old-fashioned fist fight.

Freddy's mates moved away as Freddy took a firm hold of his orb and turned it twice. He darted his eyes at William and stepped a little closer, then stopped.

William hurriedly pulled his own orb out of his jacket pocket. His heart was pounding. It felt as if it was going to jump out of his chest. He had to get control over his hands.

Suddenly Freddy flung his orb at William. It shot towards him at an insane speed.

William barely managed to fling himself down into the snow before the orb swooshed by, right over him. William rolled over and cautiously got to his knees, looking for it. Instead of crashing into the brick wall behind him, the orb had curved around like a boomerang and come flying back. In a well-practised motion, Freddy caught the orb like a professional baseball player. And before William could gather his wits, Freddy had launched the orb at him again.

Once more William had to throw himself down into the cold snow. The orb returned to Freddy and William got back to his feet. He glanced around. He noted that the rest of the group had turned up too, although he couldn't see Iscia anywhere. Everyone's attention was on him, watching in anticipation. William got the impression that they had all shown up to see the new student get it.

"What are you waiting for?" Freddy yelled. "Aren't *you* going to do anything? This is too easy."

William began to fumble with his own orb.

This time, Freddy's orb hit him in the stomach. It knocked him backwards and he hit the snow hard. He lay on his back, struggling to breathe, feeling his lungs burn, his stomach throbbing from the impact.

This was getting serious.

William looked at Freddy's orb. It hovered right over him now. As if it was waiting for further instructions from Freddy. Suddenly it shot down at him with lightning speed and crashed into his chest. The pain was so sharp that William couldn't even scream. He kicked at the orb but it darted out of reach and returned to its owner. William grabbed his chest and tried to rub the pain away. He didn't know if he could take another blow. This was not looking good.

William rolled over onto his stomach and lay in the deep snow until he could get control over his breath again. The cold snow soothed his chest and he could feel himself becoming calmer as the pain receded.

He held his orb in front of him and forced himself to

concentrate. He could hear Freddy laughing.

"All you have to do is say 'surrender' and I'll stop," Freddy shouted. "I promise."

Part of William wanted to just give up. He was cold and his body felt as if it had been trampled by a herd of elephants. He lifted his head up and looked at the others. His eyes stopped at a figure standing behind the group. It was Iscia. She raised her hand and held up four fingers. William immediately understood why.

A burst of energy shot through him. He couldn't give up. Not now.

"What do you say?" shouted Freddy. "Had enough?"

"No," said William through clenched teeth. He looked down at his own orb.

"What?" said Freddy.

But William didn't answer. He had made up his mind. He was not going to give up without a fight. And he had to solve the orb to Level Four before he could fight Freddy. That's what Iscia had meant.

He focused.

The feeling started in his stomach and spread to his arms and his head. And then his fingers got to work. He could feel something whooshing over his head. It was probably Freddy's orb again. But he didn't care. All his attention was on his own orb now, which clicked and vibrated as his fingers spun it this way and that, until it finally displayed a glowing four on the screen. He had reached another level.

William looked up and saw Freddy throwing his orb towards him again. William tossed his own orb up into the air. A bright light shot out of it and formed a transparent wall in front of him. Freddy's orb smashed into the glowing shield and bounced back towards its owner.

A gasp went through the small crowd as the orb hit Freddy in the stomach so hard he fell backwards into the snow. The orb hovered over him. One of the boys tried to help him up, but he tore loose from his grip.

"Let go," Freddy sneered as he stood up.

Meanwhile William had got to his feet and was standing waiting. He could see the others. Their expressions had changed now, as if they didn't understand what was going on. He looked at Iscia.

"Watch out!" she cried.

Freddy's orb was heading towards him again.

William dodged out of the way and threw his orb into the air a second time. The glowing wall appeared again and a loud *ZAP!* was heard as Freddy's orb crashed into it. But this time it didn't bounce back. It seemed to be stuck in the wall. It smoked and hummed before exploding into hundreds of tiny pieces that scattered in the snow.

William looked at his own orb, which was still hovering above him. The bright light disappeared. He held out his hand and the orb dropped into his palm.

He looked up at Freddy staring back at him, speechless.

"B-b-but how…?" he stammered. His face was almost as white as the snow. His friends pulled him away and they disappeared around the corner of the building.

William's eyes searched for Iscia. But she was gone.

Big snowflakes wafted down over the large open area behind the Institute. William shivered as he walked away. Rows of majestic trees towered over him on both sides of the footpath.

He glanced down at the orb in his hand. He was on Level Four now. It was as if his orb had understood that he needed help. Or as if he and the orb had helped each other. He tucked it well down into his jacket pocket, wondering what other secrets the little sphere might be hiding.

William stopped. He suddenly felt as if someone was watching him. He looked up and spotted Iscia standing under one of the big trees.

"William," she called, waving him over.

As he approached, she retreated towards the trunk of the large tree and gestured for him to follow suit. The long, snow-covered branches hung over them and hid them completely from the windows in the building up ahead.

"Thanks," she said.

"What for?" William asked, surprised.

"For putting Freddy in his place. He had that coming."

"I think I wrecked his orb," William said. He felt a little guilty about that.

"Relax," Iscia snorted. "It'll be repaired. Worst-case scenario, he'll get a new one. Then he'd have to start all over again – from scratch." Iscia smiled with a wry glint in her eye. Then she held out her hand to William. "Friends?"

William stared at her hand as if it were a creature from another planet.

"Friends?" she repeated.

He took her hand. It was warm. "Friends," he said and smiled.

CHAPTER 22

William slept like a log the whole night, and when he woke, his feelings of guilt at destroying Freddy's orb were gone. The other boy ignored him all through breakfast. *Sometimes it's good to fight fire with fire,* William thought.

After breakfast they were given their schedule for the day. The first item on the agenda was cosmological problem-solving with Professor Maple.

The oak door of the Cosmotorium slid open and an old, stooped woman in a striped dress hobbled in, supporting herself on a stick. She was the oldest professor at the Institute, and moved like a tortoise. Iscia had warned William about her at breakfast.

"Take your seats!" Professor Maple called in a reedy voice.

William watched as she stopped in front of the stairs that led up to the small podium where her desk was located.

"Do you think she's going to make it?" he whispered.

"Wait and see," Iscia responded from over his shoulder.

The students moved to their places and waited. Professor Maple stood still for a moment, then clapped and raised her arms out to the sides as if she were planning to fly up the stairs. Suddenly two robot arms dropped down from the ceiling. Like a parent lifting a small toddler, the robot arms picked up the old woman and carried her across to the podium, positioning her above the chair before setting her down gently and vanishing again just as quickly as they had appeared.

"Well, what are you waiting for? Sit down!" Professor Maple called, waving her stick at the class.

William took a seat and looked around. The ceiling was painted with stars and planets. Tall shelves filled with globes lined the walls. Some of the globes were as small as apples while others were the size of beach balls.

"We'll pick up where we left off last week," Professor Maple announced, pressing a button on her desk.

A small, square box with three small lenses hummed above her. A light flared up in the lenses and then disappeared again.

"Damned projector! Haven't they looked at it yet?" grunted the professor, raising her cane.

She whacked the machine a couple of times. The light came on again and she lowered her stick. Suddenly the projector fell off the ceiling and lurched towards the old woman.

"Watch out!" William called before he had a chance to think.

But instead of crashing into her head, the projector veered

to the side and continued into the room. It spun around a couple of times before swooping down towards the floor and then up into the air again.

"Stop showing off," the professor chided the machine, rapping on her desk.

The projector composed itself and then settled calmly in the air above them, humming faintly. William stared at the little box in fascination.

The light came back on in the lenses and a three-dimensional planet appeared in front of them in mid-air. The planet grew in both size and brightness until it was as big as a basketball. Then it began to rotate. To William it looked like a small sun. Then a new planet appeared next to the burning sun. The new planet was smaller, and grey with dark spots. It started orbiting the larger one. *Mercury*, William thought to himself.

One planet after another appeared and began orbiting, and William realized that he was looking at the solar system with the sun in the middle. Then the solar system shrank in scale and another came into view.

William looked up at the galaxy slowly rotating above them, and thought about how the Earth wasn't actually all that big. And that if his grandfather was somewhere on such a small planet, William ought to be able to find him.

"Get started," Professor Maple called, snapping William out of his daydream.

He saw the planets heading towards him. The galaxies multiplied, one descending to hover in front of each candidate.

"You have one hour to recreate the Milky Way," Professor Maple said before pressing another button on her desk. A screen appeared in front of her.

"And now we'll make some wonderful chocolate cupcakes as easy as one-two-three," a silken voice announced from her monitor.

William sat on a bench out in the garden eating the lunch he had made for himself in the cafeteria that morning. The rest of the candidates were sitting with Freddy a little way off. Every once in a while, Freddy would whisper something and point at William. The others in the group would snicker and chuckle.

"They're a bunch of idiots," a voice behind William said, and Iscia sat down next to him. "They couldn't find south if they were at the North Pole," she continued. "I noticed you finished your solar system. Why didn't you say anything to Professor Maple? You could have scored some bonus points with her."

"I don't know," William said, looking down at his lunch.

Having lived for so long in hiding, he wasn't used to letting people see that he was good at things. Nor had he ever really felt the need to prove anything. But with Iscia it was different. He wanted to show her what he could do. He was glad she'd noticed that he'd finished early.

"Look over there," Iscia said, pointing at Professor Maple, who was just leaving the Cosmotorium. She locked the door behind her, put the key in her pocket, and then shuffled away across the open area, supporting herself on her cane. She was holding a stack of grey folders under her arm. Iscia kept her eyes on the folders as Professor Maple passed them.

"Do you see those folders?" Iscia whispered.

"Mmm," William said.

"I wish I could get my hands on them."

"What are they for?" William asked, getting up.

"I don't really know. But the teachers are always writing in them. I'm guessing, but I think they're full of information about us. I've asked to see my folder loads of times, but they just say no. I think the Institute actually knows more about us than we do." She stood up, brushing the snow off the seat of her trousers. "I'd really like to know where they're planning to send me. I'm sure that's in the folder," she said thoughtfully.

"Send you?" William asked.

"Every year some of the candidates are sent away. I don't know why. Everything is kept secret. Not even the ones going know where they're headed."

"You're kidding, right?" William was shocked.

But Iscia was deadly serious. "No, I'm not kidding. And I have a feeling that it won't be long before I'm sent away," she said.

"And you think that's in your folder?"

"I'm not entirely sure. I hope so," Iscia said.

"Where do they keep the folders when they're not in use?" William asked.

Iscia shook her head. "I've heard they lock them in a room they call the Archive. But I don't know where it is. I've only heard rumours. I don't even know if there *is* an archive."

William thought about this, a secret archive full of information. That was exactly what he needed now. Based on what Slapperton had told him, he was convinced that the Institute had answers about his grandfather and why he'd run off with the luridium.

"We need a map or a floor plan," William said, scratching his head.

"The projector!" Iscia said suddenly.

"What do you mean?"

"Professor Maple's projector has maps and holographic models of pretty much everything. Maybe it has something for the Institute?"

"Let's borrow it," William said, pulling Iscia along with him towards the Cosmotorium. Come on!"

CHAPTER 23

The Cosmotorium door swung open silently and William peered into the dark room. The projector was still hanging from the ceiling over Professor Maple's desk. William slipped inside and waved to Iscia. She stuck her head through the doorway and looked around sceptically.

"I don't like this," she whispered.

"It'll be fine. Come on," William said, handing her a hair grip.

"How did you learn to pick locks?" she asked, sticking the grip back in her hair.

"I read about it in a book," he said.

Iscia was frowning at the projector. "If we get it down, we have to take it somewhere else. There's a guard here," she said, peering around nervously.

"We have to get it down first," William said, stopping next to the teacher's desk.

He spotted a button in the right-hand corner. He pushed

it. The projector began to hum, but it didn't move.

"Why's it just hovering there? We need to get it to come down!"

William looked around. He had an idea. He pointed to the two arms hanging from the ceiling right over the whiteboard behind the desk.

"We just have to clap, right?"

He clapped twice. The robot arms twitched before coming to life and running along a track in the ceiling. They stopped right above them and grabbed Iscia, lifting her up off the floor.

"Not me!" she wailed.

But it was too late. Soon she was suspended, dangling in the air above William.

"Sorry," William said. "I thought they would take me. See if you can grab the projector since you're up there." He hid a smile.

"I'm really not a fan of heights," Iscia whispered.

"Do you want to get into the Archive or not?"

Iscia closed her eyes for a moment. When she opened them again, she seemed calmer.

"OK, take me to the projector," she announced loudly and clearly to the strong metal arms holding her.

The arms transported her across the room, squeaking to a halt right in front of the projector.

"Try to get it down," William said.

Iscia cautiously took hold of the little projector and pulled it down. She held it out in front of her, arms outstretched, as if it was a stinky, old sock.

"Put me on the floor again," she instructed without taking her eyes off the projector. The arms twitched again and transported her back, setting her down next to William. "We have to get out of here before somebody notices us," she said, handing him the projector.

William and Iscia were soon walking rapidly through the large park behind the Institute. Iscia kept glancing around as if she expected someone to discover them at any moment.

"We have to find a place where we can work without anyone seeing us," William said, patting the projector that was now hidden under his jacket.

"In here," Iscia said, pulling him towards the cybernetic garden.

"What about the man-eating plants?" William hissed.

"Just do as I say and you'll be fine," Iscia said. "I just let a set of mechanical arms fling me around. I'm sure you can deal with a little greenhouse."

"Greenhouse, huh?" William said, eyeing the conservatory looming ahead of them.

They stopped in front of the enormous iron doors that led into the garden.

William had absolutely no desire to go in there, not after what had happened last time, but he was going to have to trust

Iscia. Right now, his need to find out about his grandfather trumped his fear of the plants.

Iscia pulled her orb out of her jacket pocket and placed it in the hollow spot in the middle of the heavy iron door. It swung open.

"Are you coming?" she asked.

William stared at the seemingly harmless grassy lawn a little way inside.

"The grass is safe as long as you don't step on it," Iscia said. "And the most dangerous plants are in cages. Just don't get too close to them."

William took a deep breath, relaxed his shoulders and exhaled. That made him feel a bit better.

He followed Iscia in among the tall trees and perilous plants. Some of them bared their teeth at them as they passed. Others turned away as if they weren't interested.

"Looks like they've just been fed," Iscia said, pointing to a plant that was lying with its mouth wide open, snoring.

Iscia turned onto a narrower path. William jogged to catch up. They followed the winding path deeper into the gigantic greenhouse until they came to a large hedge with a door in the middle. Iscia opened it and went through, William following close behind her.

There were no bars and no plants snapping at them in here, just a large, open space. Three benches were set around a fountain with a statue of a woman in the middle. She was holding a copper clock above her head.

"Aren't they cute?" Iscia said, pointing down into the water.

William stopped next to her. He could see colourful fish gliding by just beneath the surface. One of the fish stuck its head out and looked at them.

"They like it when you pet them," Iscia said.

"Are you sure?"

"Yeah. Pat that one on the head."

William leaned over and reached his hand out. He was about to touch the fish when it suddenly spat out a long stream of water that hit him full in the face. William leaped back spluttering. Iscia laughed so hard she had to sit down on one of the benches.

"That wasn't funny," William muttered.

"Are you kidding? It was hilarious," Iscia hiccupped, wiping her eyes.

They sat for a while without saying anything.

"It's very quiet in here," William said.

"Yes, very." Iscia suddenly grew serious, turning to face William and pointing at his jacket. "Let's get this over with," she said.

William carefully put his hand into his jacket and pulled out the projector. "How do we even turn it on – there's no button?" he said, turning it over.

"Professor Maple usually bangs on it when it acts up," Iscia said.

"Then let's do that," William said, rapping on it a couple of times. Nothing happened.

William tried again, harder this time. Still nothing.

"Maybe there's some other way to find out where the Archive is," Iscia suggested. "Let's just take this back and try something else."

"Yeah, OK – the projector's probably broken," William said.

He went to stand up when Iscia suddenly cried, "Look – a light!" She was pointing at the lenses.

Then the projector started humming, and before William had a chance to react, it shot up into the air. He was so startled, he forgot to let go. The projector pulled him up with it, dangerously high, William dangling underneath, leaving Iscia standing way down below.

"Let go!" she called, pacing back and forth. "Aim for the fountain. I'm sure it's deep enough!"

William shook his head and closed his eyes.

"It's trying to shake you off!" he heard Iscia yelling.

William clung on as hard as he could. Suddenly the projector dived downwards. William opened his eyes just as he struck a big rosebush. Sharp thorns jabbed him all over. Then the projector did a U-turn and swooped back up again and over the hedge into the main part of the conservatory. Once there, it began to dive-bomb all the cages until it reached a plant William recognized immediately. It was the green octopus vine that had devoured a bird last time he was here. Its long tentacle arms started twisting up towards him.

William shook the projector. "Get us away! It's going to eat us both!"

But the projector didn't budge. One of the tentacles was just beneath them now. It was reaching for William's feet. There was a click from inside the projector and the lights in the lenses went out. They started losing height.

"No, not now!" William cried.

He looked down and saw that Iscia had stopped right outside the plant's cage. She was looking up at him, her eyes wide with horror.

"Do something!" he cried.

"Like what?" she yelled back, panic-stricken.

"Anything!"

The first tentacle took hold of one of his legs and started tightening itself around it. "It's got me!" William screamed.

The green tentacle dragged him down further. Another tentacle twined around his hips. The projector hummed to life again and started pulling upwards, but the vine grabbed it and pulled it down. Soon the plant's green tentacles surrounded William and the projector, grasping and curling around its prey.

William stopped struggling.

He looked down at a dark mouth in the ground, remembering how the bird had been chewed to bits and its remains spat out again. In a few seconds the same thing was going to happen to him.

Suddenly he remembered his orb. He manoeuvred it out of his pocket. "Can you help me?" he whispered.

One of the tentacles instantly shot up and thwacked the orb out of his hand. "No!" William cried as his orb fell into the dark mouth beneath him.

Then everything went completely still. The tentacles stopped moving. William hung there, waiting. Sweat poured down his face and his heart was hammering so hard it felt as if it would pound right through his ribcage.

"What's going on?" Iscia yelled from somewhere on the other side of the green tentacles.

The plant started coughing and clearing its throat and suddenly the dark mouth spat out the orb. It hung there – unharmed – in front of William.

"Are you going to help me or not?" William said, as if he expected it to suddenly talk back at him.

But the orb just continued to hover. William could feel the tentacles tighten around his chest. Soon he wouldn't be able to breathe. In sheer desperation, he grabbed the orb and started beating at the tentacle round his chest.

William felt the tentacle loosen its grip. He was finally able to inhale, filling his lungs with air. He could feel his strength returning with the oxygen. He looked down at the huge plant. It seemed like it could feel pain.

"Do it on the others!" he heard Iscia call out.

William kept beating at the vine. For every blow, he could feel the green tentacles letting go. Little by little. He kept hammering desperately until he suddenly dropped to the ground, landing right beside the gaping mouth. The projector bounced off a leaf next to him. William managed to grab it before it tumbled into the darkness.

Soon afterwards, William and Iscia were back on the bench again. Aside from a couple of scrapes on his forehead and several rips to his jacket, William had emerged unharmed.

"Remind me, would you, not to come in here with you again!" William said.

Iscia smiled and poked him in the side with her elbow. "But you won! You conquered one of the most dangerous plants they have in here."

"Doesn't matter. I've already used up all my chances in this garden," William said.

"I think it likes you now," Iscia said, patting the projector, which was hovering next to William. It was rubbing against his shoulder and purring like a cat.

"Maybe it just needs to be tamed?" he said with a wry smile.

"Hmm. Maybe," Iscia said.

"We need a map of the Institute," William said, looking expectantly at the projector.

The projector pulled away and hung in the air as if it were

contemplating what William had just said. Suddenly a hologram of the Milky Way appeared in front of them.

"No, not the Milky Way, the *Institute*," William said.

The hologram of the Milky Way disappeared, replaced by a map of London.

Iscia leaned towards the projector. "The In-sti-tute!" she said, enunciating loudly and clearly.

A new image appeared in front of them, an architectural drawing.

"Gotcha!" Iscia cried.

They sat and looked at the image hovering in the air in front of them.

"Wow, look at all those rooms!" Iscia exclaimed. "This place is a lot bigger than I thought."

She pointed to the text at the top of the map.

Institute for Post-Human Research
Founded 1967

"Here's the main building," William said.

"And there's Goffman's office," Iscia said.

"But what's that right there?" William asked, pointing to a fairly sizeable area behind the office.

"It doesn't say," Iscia said.

"Could that be the Archive?"

"If it is, we might as well forget the whole thing," she said in disappointment. "No one enters Goffman's office without permission."

Neither spoke for a while.

"We'll do it tonight," William finally said, nodding his head decisively.

"Are you crazy?" Iscia asked.

"I thought you wanted to know what it says in your folder?"

"Well, yes…" she admitted.

"And I need to find out about my grandfather. I think they know more than they're telling me," William said.

"About your grandfather?" Iscia said.

William didn't answer. He didn't know where to start. Finally he said, "Do you know what luridium is?"

"Luridium?" she repeated.

"Yes," William said. "Have you heard of it?"

Iscia shook her head. "Never. What a weird name. What is it?"

"I'll tell you more tonight," he said, getting up. "Let's meet in the dining hall at ten."

Iscia remained seated. The idea of breaking into Goffman's office clearly scared her.

But William knew he couldn't stop now. Not when they were so close to finding a whole archive full of secret information.

CHAPTER 24

It was 10.12 p.m. William crept down the stairs to the ground floor as quickly as he could. He was late because his door had stubbornly refused to let him out, lecturing him instead about how it was too late to leave his room, and it wasn't safe to run around the Institute at night. You never knew what you might run into. William had had to use all his persuasive abilities before the door eventually, grudgingly, let him out. Now he just hoped Iscia hadn't had second thoughts.

When he reached the bottom step, William stopped and listened. Darkness lay like a black fog over the hallway. He was alone. A solitary wall lamp gave off just enough light for William to see where to go.

William made his way down the hallway, which led to the dining hall. He stopped next to a bronze statue that resembled the Statue of Liberty and peered around him.

"Iscia," he whispered.

The only thing he heard in response was a faint echo of his

own voice. Iscia had probably been here and left again when he hadn't appeared on time. William was trying to decide whether or not to go back to his room too, when a creaking sound made him turn. A silhouette was moving along the hallway. Holding his breath, William squeezed in between the wall and the statue. The silhouette was coming closer.

It was the same old woman he'd seen before, in the hallway outside his room. She was pushing a trolley full of buckets, brooms and rags. William pressed himself against the wall. No one could know he was out wandering the hallways at this hour. The woman stopped right next to the statue. He could see her clearly now. She was very old. Her skin was grey and wrinkled and she wore her hair up in a little hairnet. A small, mechanical hummingbird sat on her shoulder grooming its feathers. She looked around, then carried on down the hallway, finally disappearing around a corner.

William didn't dare come out from behind the statue until the sound of the cleaning trolley's squeaking wheels had completely gone. If Iscia didn't show up, should he try to find the Archive alone? No, he needed her. She knew the Institute much better than he did.

"Psst!" he heard from somewhere in the darkness. William stopped. It had to be Iscia.

"Here … up the stairs."

William saw a narrow staircase a little way down the hallway. It was blocked off with a chain, and hanging from the chain was a brass sign that read: *Employees Only*.

"Hurry up," the voice whispered.

Iscia was waiting halfway up the stairs, concealed from view. William stepped over the chain and climbed up to her.

"You're late."

"I was negotiating a curfew with my door," he explained.

"So what time does the little one need to be back, then?" Iscia said sarcastically.

William ignored her and continued up the staircase.

Soon they were on the first floor, peering down a long, white hallway that seemed to go on for ever.

"You lead the way. I've never been to Goffman's office," William said.

The hallway was so blindingly white that it was hard to see where the floor ended and the walls began. William ran his hand along the smooth wall to keep a straight course.

"There it is," Iscia said as they turned a corner.

In front of them was a white door with no knob or handle. It almost blended into the wall.

"How do we get in?" William asked.

"No idea," Iscia responded. "You're the genius here."

William ran his hand over the door's smooth surface. No doorknob or handle or keyhole. Then he stopped, and almost had to smile.

"Could it be so easy?" he murmured.

"What are you talking about?" Iscia said.

"The new fridge we got last year had no handle," William said, pushing in on the door.

The door gave a quiet *click* and swung open.

"Things aren't always so complicated," he said with a smile.

"But why doesn't Goffman's door have a lock?" Iscia asked suspiciously.

"Don't know. Maybe because he's the boss and he doesn't think anyone would dare to break into his office," William said, peering around cautiously. "Come on!"

CHAPTER 25

Goffman's office was nearly empty. A large white desk sat in the middle of the room. Resting on it was an old-fashioned globe.

"I can't see any door into the Archive," Iscia said.

"Don't give up so quickly," William said, heading further into the room. He stopped when he felt the familiar vibration in his body, starting in the pit of his stomach. He relaxed his shoulders and closed his eyes.

"Um, what are you doing?" Iscia asked.

"Shh," he said, concentrating on the darkness beneath his eyelids.

He felt the vibrations increasing. Soon they were travelling up his spine and out to his arms and head. When he opened his eyes again, he saw it immediately: glowing symbols hovering in the air over the globe – some were bigger than others and glowing more brightly.

"Do you see anything?" he heard Iscia ask. She sounded far away.

One of the symbols increased in intensity, as did a letter *X*, which had settled on top of what must be north on the globe. William spun the globe so the glowing symbol was directly over the *X*. He heard a *click*. The symbol disappeared and a new one appeared. He did the same again. Another distant *click*.

"What's going on?" Iscia asked, leaning on the desk.

And now William felt it, too: the whole office was vibrating.

"I don't like this," Iscia whispered.

"We're moving," William said, staring at a ballpoint pen rolling across the desk. "The whole room is moving."

"Like a lift?" Iscia asked.

And just as quickly as the vibrations had begun, they stopped. William and Iscia stood, listening, but nothing happened.

"What do we do now?" she whispered, inching closer to him. William surveyed the room.

"Could it be…?" he muttered to himself and headed back towards the door.

He put his hand on the cold surface and pushed carefully. The door swung open and Iscia gasped.

They were now staring into pitch darkness. A cool draught hit them.

"I'm not sure about this," Iscia said. "I've heard so many stories…"

But William knew that he had no choice. If he was going to find out more about his grandfather, there was only one thing to do. He walked through the doorway into the darkness. He could hear a faint humming way up ahead; otherwise it was completely quiet.

"We're in this together," Iscia said, stepping through and shutting the door behind them. William smiled.

Suddenly they began to hear clicking above them, and soon hundreds of light bulbs started blinking on like fireworks. Then the clicking subsided.

"Wow!" Iscia exclaimed, rubbing her eyes to get used to the light.

A vast, white room revealed itself before them. The ceiling had to be twenty metres high, and the space was filled with endless rows of shelves that towered over them.

The ceiling was covered with small vents, and a display on the wall next to them showed the humidity in the room.

"What if what we're looking for is way up there?" Iscia asked, pointing to the highest shelves.

"There must be some way of getting up there," William said, peering around. His eyes stopped at a sign that hung from the closest archive shelf. *Beware of Laika*, it said in large, hand-written letters. "Who's Laika?" He glanced at Iscia.

"Beats me, but I don't like it…" She trailed off. "Shh," she whispered.

They stood and listened.

"There it is again," she whispered.

And now William heard it too – a faint echo of something moving somewhere in the stacks.

"It's getting closer," he said, taking a few steps backwards.

Suddenly two stepladders on wheels – one black, the other grey – came zipping out from behind one of the shelves. Each one was a concertina-like construction with a platform at the top. These must be for getting up to the higher parts of the tall shelves, William realized.

The stepladders were rolling towards them at a crazy speed. It was almost as if they were racing each other. The black stepladder cut the other one off, trying to push it into one of the shelves. They swerved on screeching tyres, almost losing control, then stopped right in front of William and Iscia.

"Pick me!" the stepladders cried in unison. "Pick me!"

"Wait a second," the black stepladder said. "There's two of them."

"Two of them?" the grey one said.

"Yes, two of them," the black one said.

The stepladders went quiet, as if this was information they had to contemplate for a moment.

"Pick me!" the black one said.

"No, pick me," the grey one said.

"Pick me!" they yelled in unison.

"What kind of bots are you?" William asked.

"We're stepbrothers," one of the stepladders explained.

146

"No, we're not," the other said. "We're in no way related."

"What are you, then?" said William impatiently.

"Vertical-bots," the stepladders said at the same time. "We'll drive you wherever you want, whenever you want and however high you want."

"Perfect. We'll take one each," William said, glancing at Iscia.

"Pick me! Pick me!" the stepladders said again.

Iscia hesitated.

William hopped up onto the black stepladder. "Come on. It'll be fun," he said.

She rolled her eyes and climbed up onto the first rung of the grey stepladder.

"Where to?" the stepladders yelled.

William smiled. The ladders seemed completely desperate to be of use. Maybe they were starved of company? No doubt it was terribly lonely here in the enormous archives.

"Iscia would like her folder and I would like to know more about Tobias Wenton," William said.

"Ugh, boring. We have a lot of material in here that's way more fun than that," said the stepladder William was standing on. "Couldn't you choose something else? We have three full aisles about the Industrial Revolution."

"Or moon-landing conspiracy theories," the other one interjected.

"Sounds exciting," William said firmly, "but not today."

"OK!" cried the black ladder, zooming off so quickly its wheels squealed.

"Let's meet back here once we've found what we need," William called to Iscia before the ladders each turned in different directions and shot into the stacks.

"All right," Iscia called back, sounding less than thrilled.

William's stepladder was moving extremely fast. He climbed up a couple more rungs so he could see where they were going. He had to hold on tightly with both hands. The stepladder turned right and then left and then continued straight ahead at top speed. Suddenly it screeched to a halt.

"Tobias Wenton," the stepladder announced in a monotone.

William looked around. They were in the very heart of the vast archives. One of the lights overhead wasn't working, so it was a little darker here. A thick layer of dust covered the folders in front of him. This did not appear to be the most frequently visited part of the Archive.

"Is this whole shelf about Tobias Wenton?" William asked hopefully.

"No," the ladder replied curtly.

"Where is Tobias Wenton's folder?" William asked.

"Higher up," the ladder said, continuing to move upwards.

William cast a quick glance down. They were already staggeringly high. He focused on the folders on the shelves, and suddenly the ladder jerked to a halt. It stood and swayed alarmingly back and forth before it stabilized.

"Professor Wenton," the ladder declared.

William spotted a folder that had *TW* written by hand on its spine. He pulled it out and blew the dust off before opening it. His heart almost stopped at the sight of what was in it. Or, to be more precise, what *wasn't* in it. Because apart from an old photograph, the folder was completely empty. William pulled out the picture and put the folder back where it belonged. He gasped when he realized what the picture was of. Why in the world…?

A sound made him look up. He hurriedly shoved the picture into his pocket. He was not alone.

CHAPTER 26

William heard sharp claws scraping against the floor below him.

"What's that?" he exclaimed. He couldn't see anything from the top of the stepladder.

"What's what?" the vertical-bot asked.

"That sound. It sounded like … an animal…?"

"Probably Laika," the ladder said.

"Laika," William repeated. He remembered the sign hanging by the entrance. "Who's Laika?"

The ladder didn't respond. Something scratched past on the other side of the shelf.

"Is Laika dangerous?" William asked.

"Only when you get too close," the ladder said.

"I have what I need," William told it. "Find Iscia and get us out of here."

Then the lights went out.

In the pitch black, the only sound was William's own heart, which was beating like a galloping horse. Then he heard something moving below him again, sharp claws on the hard stone floor. Then that something stopped right beneath him.

William remembered how high he was. He cautiously leaned over the edge of the ladder and peered down.

Then he saw it.

Two yellow eyes glowed at him from the darkness below. He heard a long, deep growl. William drew back and held his breath.

"Please… Please, go away," he whispered quietly to himself.

Then there was a popping sound from the ceiling above him. One light after another came on, and soon the whole Archive was bathed in light again. He looked down. The yellow eyes had gone.

"Get me out of here!" William cried.

"Are you sure you don't want to take a peek at the Industrial Revolution?" the ladder tried.

"Completely sure," William said.

The rungs jerked and the ladder lowered itself back down to the floor again. William looked around nervously. No sign of Laika, whoever Laika might be. Soon the ladder was zooming through the tall shelves again at breakneck speed, back the way they had come.

They rounded a corner and William saw Iscia standing on her stepladder about halfway up one of the shelves. She was staring at the folder open in front of her. She must have found what she'd been looking for.

"Stop!" William instructed his ladder.

The wheels screeched as the ladder skidded sideways and stopped next to Iscia.

"Did you find it?" William asked.

"Mm," she said, without looking up.

"Is something wrong?" William asked. She seemed to be acting a little strange – evasive, even.

She closed the folder firmly and tucked it under her jacket. Still without looking at him. He decided that he would ask her later. They had more urgent matters to deal with.

"There's something in here called Laika. I think it's best we get out of here," he said, glancing behind him fearfully.

"Laika?" she asked, and finally met his eyes.

"Yeah, with glowing eyes," William said. "Let's go."

He was about to tell the vertical-bot to step on it, but stopped when he spotted something out of the corner of his eye. He turned his head and saw her: the old woman.

She was standing by a shelf a short distance away, completely still, staring at him with cold eyes. The little hummingbird was still sitting on her shoulder.

"Iscia," he whispered, without taking his eyes off the old woman. Iscia turned and saw her too.

"What do we do now?" she mouthed back.

"I'll count to three, then I'll pull you over onto my ladder. Your stepladder will block the aisle so she won't be able to follow us," William whispered as he leaned out and took hold of her arm. "One ... two ... three!"

Iscia jumped.

"Go!" William commanded his ladder. The old lady began to walk towards them.

"Where to?" the ladder asked.

"Anywhere, as long as it's out of here!" William yelled back. "Quick!"

"Out it is, then!" The ladder was already backing up, then it turned abruptly and zoomed off.

William looked back at the old woman, who had started running now. "The ladder should stop her," William cried, glancing at Iscia's ladder, which was blocking the space between the shelves. "That's it – any minute—"

He broke off as the old woman jumped over it and kept coming towards them, faster and faster.

"OK. This isn't going to go well," he muttered to himself.

Suddenly the old woman split in half at the middle. The top half of her body separated just above her hips, dived forwards and landed on her hands. Her legs and hips picked up the pace.

"*What?*" William gasped as he stared at the two halves that were following them.

Then the two parts morphed into two men. William recognized them immediately.

It was the two red-headed drivers.

CHAPTER 27

"You two have been on a little outing, I see." Goffman was standing beside the globe in his office. William glanced over at Iscia, who was still holding her folder in her hands.

"We were just…" William began, but stopped. They'd been caught red-handed. There was no point trying to explain it away.

Goffman pointed at Iscia. "She stays," he told the man who was holding her. "Get William back to his room. I'll deal with him later."

William tried to make eye contact with Iscia, but she avoided his gaze. Why was she acting so strangely? Was it something she had seen in her folder?

"Welcome back. You got caught, I understand?" the door said, shutting again behind William.

William crossed the room without answering.

"You think it was me, don't you? I can assure you that I had nothing to do with it," the door said apologetically.

"You were the only one who knew I had gone out," William said, annoyed.

"That's a little naïve," the door said. "The Institute has eyes and ears everywhere. I don't understand how you managed to get as far as you did before you were caught. What were you looking for?"

William pulled the photo out of his pocket.

"It doesn't matter. The folder I was after was almost empty in any case. And then those two guys who brought me here showed up. First they were an old woman, then she split in two. I don't think they're human."

"Hybrids," the door said.

"Hybrids?" William repeated. "As in part-human and part-machine? Like the plants in the garden?"

"Something like that," the door said. "There are a few of them here at the Institute. So advanced that it's impossible to tell the difference between them and regular people."

William was surprised. "Like who?" he asked.

"No idea. It's strictly secret. Only a few—" The door stopped as an alarm started wailing somewhere in the building. "Strange," the door muttered to itself.

"What's going on?" William asked.

"Don't know. Nobody mentioned a fire drill. Must be something important, though," the door said.

William sat down on the bed and looked at the photo.

He recognized the subject. It was the old desk he'd inherited from his grandfather. Someone must have emptied out his grandfather's folder. But had they forgotten to take the photo? Or was this a message ... from his grandfather?

Suddenly the door opened, and one of the drivers marched in. He came right over to William, picked him up and slung him over his shoulder.

The gate to the cybernetic garden opened and the red-headed man proceeded inside with William still flung over his shoulder. The alarm wailed in the distance.

The plants reached for them and hissed. The man hissed back, and the plants retreated in fear. Where were they going? Was he about to become plant food?

They made straight for the oasis in the middle of the conservatory. Once they were inside, the red-headed man set William down and went to stand beside the other driver.

Fritz Goffman took a step forward. Beside him was one of the strangest creatures William had ever seen. Its body was made of gleaming metal but it had the head of a real dog.

William recognized those glowing yellow eyes right away. This couldn't be anything other than the thing that had been trying to get him in the Archive.

Goffman patted the creature on the head. "I understand you met Laika earlier."

William nodded.

Another alarm began to sound not far from where they were. "Why are the alarms going off?" William asked.

Goffman didn't respond. He looked up at the clock that sat in the hands of the statue in the fountain. It seemed as if he was waiting for something. It was only now that William detected something he hadn't expected to see in Goffman's eyes.

Fear.

Something was very wrong.

He jumped when the door suddenly opened and Professor Slapperton stumbled in, out of breath.

"It's i-i-inside the Institute," he stuttered.

"It knows he's here," Goffman said, glancing at William.

"What knows?" William asked, his voice trembling.

And then William heard a sound he'd heard before. Something he would never forget.

Branches snapping and heavy clanking steps that thundered through the garden. Getting closer. Whatever was coming towards them was the same thing that had attacked his house back in Norway.

"Come on!" Goffman yelled, waving to William. Slapperton jumped up into the fountain. The fish swam to the side, and a couple of them stuck their heads up out of the water and spat at him. But Slapperton wasn't concerned about spitting fish right now. He grabbed the statue's arm and pulled down with all his might. There was a loud scream and something came hurtling towards them through the air. One of the cannibalistic plants crashed to the ground right next to William and lay there writhing.

"Hurry!" yelled Goffman, stepping into the fountain. Laika whimpered and jumped in behind him.

The two red-headed men did the same. One of them stopped beside William, eyeing Goffman with a look that said, *Do you want me to drag him?*

William hurriedly climbed into the fountain.

He'd had enough of being thrown around for one day.

CHAPTER 28

A solid iron hatch closed over the little group, who stood in silence while the fountain lift took them down into the darkness, deeper and deeper. William wondered how far they were going. He glanced around at the others. The silence was unbearable. He had to break it.

"What about Iscia?" William looked up at Goffman.

"What about her?" Goffman asked in return.

"Is she in danger?"

"She's safe with the others."

The lift jerked to a stop and a wall in front of them opened.

"This way!" Goffman said.

Laika bounded after him. Slapperton gestured for William to follow. And soon they were hurrying down a long hallway without any doors or windows. William's ears needed to pop. He tried swallowing, but that didn't help.

After a while, they came to a stop in front of a massive door that looked like the kind you would find in a bomb shelter.

Slapperton held his thumb in front of a sensor on the wall and the door slid open.

"Welcome, Professor Slapperton," said a voice that William thought he recognized.

"Thanks, Malin," Slapperton said, stepping into the room. He turned to William. "Welcome to the Institute's Ultra-Secret Department. Follow me."

They were surrounded by machines of every conceivable size and shape. Some of them were labelled: *Degenerator, Shrinkomat, Time Squeezer, Anti-Matter Developer.* William followed Slapperton past a rusty barrel that said *Past Turbine* and stopped.

A new door came into view ahead of them: *To the vacuum train,* it read. Slapperton raised his thumb to the fingerprint sensor on the wall. No reaction.

"Just my luck," he said, panic creeping into his voice. He tried again.

"Is something wrong?" Goffman asked.

Slapperton tried his other thumb. Still no response. "It's not working," he said. "Someone must have—"

Then the lights went out.

The little group stood there in the pitch black. There was a thundering blast above them. "It's in," Slapperton whispered. "This way," he continued, pointing a small torch into the darkness.

He pulled open a red fire door. William and the others

160

were right behind him. Slapperton shone the light into the darkness, revealing a narrow stairway down. A new boom shook the stairs.

Just as the group reached the bottom, the whole thing exploded above them. William looked up and saw flames and smoke surging down the stairway.

"Hurry!" Slapperton yelled, pointing to a train carriage up ahead.

William looked around. They had reached some kind of subterranean platform.

"Get in!" Slapperton shouted.

On the inside it was like a normal train. There were two rows of seats, one on each side. But the seats looked more like the ones you'd find in a racing car, with deep headrests and harness-style seatbelts.

"Buckle up!" Slapperton directed, sitting down in the front by the controls. The walls of the train were shaking.

"It's right outside!" Goffman cried.

Slapperton pushed two red buttons at the same time and leaned back.

"Let's hope this works," he said, closing his eyes. "Hold on tight and lean your head back against the headrest."

A new boom hit the wall right beside William. Then they heard a deep rumble followed by a loud *whoosh*, and they were pressed back into their seats. The acceleration was so violent that William couldn't move.

A short while later, the pressure let up and everything normalized again. William sat up cautiously.

"Are we moving?" he asked.

"You bet," said Slapperton. A proud smile lurked at the corner of his mouth. "We're already travelling at around five hundred miles per hour. It will stabilize at a little over a thousand."

"A thousand?" William exclaimed. He tried to imagine how fast that actually was.

"Yup," said Slapperton. "We're moving at speeds faster than an aeroplane and the speed of sound. If we weren't moving in a perfect vacuum, we would break the sound barrier when we passed seven hundred and sixty miles per hour."

"Wow," William said.

Then a scary thought hit him.

"What if we crash?" he said.

"Let's not think about that," said Slapperton.

CHAPTER 29

Professor Slapperton unbuckled his straps and stretched his legs. Laika did a couple of rounds of the carriage and then lay down at Goffman's feet, where she closed her glowing eyes and began to purr like a cat. William glanced over at the two drivers, who were sitting a short way off.

He turned to Slapperton. "What was that thing that attacked us up there?" he asked.

"A kind of machine," Slapperton replied.

"The same one that attacked my family back in Norway?" William asked.

"Probably," Slapperton said.

"A robot?"

"Yes, I suppose you could call it that. Very advanced," Slapperton said. "Once you realize it's there, it's generally too late."

"Is it ... Abraham Talley's robot?" William asked.

Slapperton and Goffman looked at each other.

"We think so," Slapperton said.

"Where are we going?" William continued.

"London," Slapperton answered. "To the safest place we can stay at this point. The Centre for Misinformation."

"Misinformation?" William repeated.

"Yes, the Centre for Misinformation is run by Professor Wellcrow. She was another of the Institute's original founders."

"I thought my grandfather founded the Institute?" William said.

"There were three people who founded the Institute. Your grandfather, Professor Wellcrow and Fritz Goffman." Slapperton leaned forward, put his elbows on his knees and looked long and seriously at William.

"I think it's time you knew what was going on," he finally said. William nodded expectantly. He completely agreed.

"Do you remember what I showed you in the cellar below the Institute?"

"Yes." William hesitated. He didn't like the idea that his grandfather had stolen something.

"The luridium that went missing?" Slapperton continued.

"Yes, I remember," William admitted.

"Well, as I told you, luridium is an intelligent metal. We don't know its precise origins, but it's very old. It can think for itself, but needs to be in contact with a living organism in order to work. That's why luridium can lie dormant for very long periods of time. Until someone finds it. I'm sure you also remember that Abraham Talley was the first person in the modern era to find a clump of luridium?"

William nodded.

"When Abraham found the luridium, it entered his body and he fell into a coma. He was taken to hospital but disappeared a couple of days later. You recall what happened to the other miners?"

"Yes," said William. He was beginning to feel impatient. They'd been through all this before. He wanted to know what had happened to his grandfather.

"When the area where the miners died was examined, the investigators discovered an ancient, impenetrable iron door covered in inscriptions," Slapperton explained. "The construction work was halted and they spent a long time trying to decipher the writing. But only a few of the symbols could be understood: *chamber* and *technology*."

Slapperton glanced at Goffman and gestured for him to carry on. Goffman cleared his throat solemnly.

"Not far from the iron door, they found a mechanical sphere … an orb. It was also covered in unintelligible symbols, none of which matched the ones on the iron door. They couldn't see any connection between them at all, and after several years they gave up trying to decipher the symbols. In sheer desperation to get through that door, they detonated a large amount of explosive, which caused sections of the tunnel system to collapse. Many lives were lost. The project was terminated, without results. The tunnel where the iron door is located was sealed up and work on the train system continued in the other tunnels."

"What happened to the orb?" William asked.

"The orb was hidden away in a vault in the cellar of an Oxford museum," Goffman said. "No one understood what it was or what it could be used for. As the years passed, both the orb and the sealed-up tunnel were forgotten."

"And what about Abraham?" William asked.

"No one knows. Until he turned up again a hundred years later, that is, at the beginning of the 1960s. He broke into the museum and tried to steal the orb. His plan failed, but once again he was able to escape.

"Your grandfather, Professor Wellcrow and I were students at Oxford at the time. We realized there must be something special about this mysterious metal sphere. It didn't have a name, so we just called it an orb.

"We started digging into the history of the orb, which led us to the history of the forgotten iron door beneath London. We even got hold of some old notes on the symbols on the door. Your grandfather managed to decipher many of them, and that's how we first heard about luridium. From what we could tell, it looked likely that there might be more luridium behind the iron door, and that the orb was actually a kind of key. When we realized how things fitted together – that the luridium had entered Abraham's body, and how dangerous it could be – we established the Institute. We wanted to protect people by containing and concealing the luridium. We kept up the search for the iron door. But we also began to follow leads throughout the world, hunting for other underground passageways, for more luridium. The small amount we found, we hid away at the Institute. We couldn't take the chance that it would end up in the wrong hands."

"What about the iron door?" William asked. "Did you find it?"

"All traces of it disappeared when London was bombed during the Second World War," Slapperton said. "But your grandfather was responsible for the orb key. And he was obsessed with the idea of finding the door. Shortly before he disappeared, he told me he had made a big breakthrough. Then you and your father were involved in that accident. Naturally he dropped everything he was working on and went to take care of you. And when he disappeared right afterwards, we lost our best chance of getting into the chamber behind the iron door."

"So you began to look for other people who could break the code and get you through the door?" William said.

"Yes," said Goffman. "We arranged codebreaking contests all over the world. And we started collecting candidates that way. The orbs at the Institute are copies of that original orb. But we also knew that you had probably inherited your grandfather's talent for codes, so we devoted a lot of resources to locating you. Who'd have guessed you were hiding in Norway?"

"Do you think my grandfather was able to open the door,

and that he's in there … somewhere?" William asked.

"That's what we're hoping," said Slapperton, and then he leaned further forward as if he was going to divulge some terrible secret. "Personally I think he found and opened the door a long time before he disappeared. For some reason or other he just didn't tell us."

"And now you want me to try to open the door?"

"First we have to find it. I think you can get your orb to show us the way," Goffman said. "It's important that we find your grandfather, but also that we gain control over any luridium that might be in there so that Abraham doesn't get hold of it. I don't need to tell you how catastrophic it would be if Abraham reached it first."

"But could my grandfather have survived for so long in there?" William said.

"That I don't know," Slapperton said. "We can only hope. Your grandfather is a clever man."

"Slowing down," Malin announced over the loudspeaker. "We will be arriving at the Centre for Misinformation in three minutes."

CHAPTER 30

Slapperton stood at a tall counter waiting for the woman seated behind it to finish on the phone. William and Goffman stood right behind him. Laika wandered around, eyes darting about nervously. She clearly didn't like this place. They were in a large room with enormous glass walls and a revolving door leading out to the street. There was a fountain towering in the middle of the room. William thought it looked like the fountain at the Institute.

The woman behind the counter finished her phone call. She set down her phone and looked up at Slapperton with a fake smile.

"Yes…?" she said.

"We're here to see Professor Wellcrow," Slapperton said.

"Sorry, but there's no one by that name working here," the woman said.

Slapperton rolled his eyes in annoyance. "Come on. Do we have to go through this charade every time I come here?"

"I've never seen you before," the woman said politely.

An irritated Slapperton shoved his hand into his jacket and pulled out a black wallet with pictures of small planets on it. He opened it and pulled out a card, which he handed to the woman. She took it, studied it for a moment, handed it back and then picked up her phone.

"Have a seat. She'll be right with you."

"Welcome, welcome," a woman's voice called out loudly.

William looked up and saw a golf cart zooming towards them. Only the cart didn't have any wheels. It glided above the smooth floor on a big black hovercraft base.

"Professor Wellcrow," called Slapperton.

The woman at the wheel smiled. She was wearing a grey striped dress and had short black hair. She wore a pair of dark sunglasses.

The golf cart did a lap around the fountain in the middle of the hall and came to an abrupt stop right in front of them.

"Jealous?" Professor Wellcrow crowed, with a sidelong glance at Slapperton. "I got it just last week."

"Hovercraft technology?" Slapperton asked.

"Anti-Isotope Hovercraft. Beta version," she said, smiling proudly.

"Of course." Slapperton nodded.

William was staring at the professor's sunglasses. A pair of thin wires ran from the rims into her forehead.

He leaned over to Goffman and whispered so she wouldn't

hear, "What kind of glasses are those?"

"She's blind, but they allow her to see," Goffman whispered back.

"Could we go somewhere we can speak in private?" Slapperton asked.

The professor's expression became serious. "Well, I see this isn't just a friendly visit," she said before turning around 180 degrees. "Climb on, gentlemen."

After a breakneck trip, the hovercart stopped at a door that read: *Anti-Audio Chamber.*

"After you," Professor Wellcrow said as the door opened and they walked in. The drivers and Laika remained outside.

The room was empty. The walls were upholstered with something that resembled sofa cushions. Wellcrow put a finger over her lips to indicate that they shouldn't speak yet. She walked over to a control panel on the wall and pushed some buttons. A quiet rushing sound poured out of speakers mounted just below the ceiling.

"Intelligent sound cancellation," she said, nodding up at the speakers. "Now it's safe to talk."

She surveyed her three visitors, her eyes coming to rest on William. "Is this him?" she asked.

"Yes," said Slapperton.

"We've met before. Did you know that?" she said.

"No," William replied, shaking his head.

"You were just a baby, a newborn. Of course, I had my eyes back then. You were a cute little thing." She paused. Then she turned to Slapperton. "What's going on?"

"It found us," Slapperton whispered.

"I figured it must be something like that," she said seriously. "I mean, we've known this day would come. Are you going to try to find the iron door?"

"Yes," Slapperton said. "But we need a place to stay until tomorrow."

Professor Wellcrow keyed in a code, and the door to the Anti-Audio Chamber opened again with a *whoosh*. "We have to get you to safety," she said, waving William out of the room.

The hovercart zoomed down the long hallway at a ridiculous speed. Professor Wellcrow pulled a phone out of her pocket and dialled a number.

"It's me. We're on our way down to the cellar. It's a Code Eleven. Yes, Code Eleven. No, this is not a drill," she said.

An alarm went off almost immediately.

Then booms could be heard as heavy doors slammed shut throughout the building. The lights in the hallway flickered and dimmed for a moment before becoming stable.

"That was us making the switchover to our internal power supply," Wellcrow explained. "We're now officially cut off from the world."

*   *   *

"We haven't needed to use these cells for a long time, but they're updated periodically," Professor Wellcrow explained as they arrived in the cellar. "You'll each get a room. They were built to keep things out, but it's easy for *you* to get out if anything should happen. There's an emergency hatch in each room that will take you right out of the building. I don't think I need to add that the hatches should only be used in an emergency," she continued.

"Of course," Slapperton said, casting a nervous glance at Goffman.

CHAPTER 31

William lay on his bed in the small cell. His eyes rested on a red hatch in the wall next to him. *EMERGENCY EXIT*, it said in large black letters. His mind was racing with all the information he'd learned on the train. He held his orb in both hands, resting on his chest. For some reason or other, he felt safer when he held it that way.

Could he trust what Slapperton and Goffman had told him? Just thinking about it made his head spin.

The mattress was hard, but he felt sleep creeping over him all the same. His thoughts turned to fog, and keeping his eyes open became a struggle until finally he let them close.

"William," a voice whispered.

William sat up in bed. He'd been sound asleep. He rubbed his eyes and squinted around the room. The silhouette of a man stood in the middle of the room. The figure was flickering slightly. Suddenly it disappeared and then reappeared.

A hologram! William thought.

"William," the voice repeated.

William stared, not quite believing his eyes. Could it really be…?

"Grandfather?" he whispered.

The hologram didn't respond. William realized that it was probably a recording. He got up and cautiously moved closer. He recognized the old man in front of him from photos. It really was his grandfather.

"William, I don't know how old you'll be when you see this, and I don't know how much you already know. But since you've come here, I'm assuming you've already found out some of the details. Let me begin with the most obvious. My name is Tobias Wenton. I'm your grandfather." He took a deep breath. "You've grown up surrounded by secrets. And I'm sure you've often wondered what's going on. It is only fair that you should be put fully in the picture. Especially since I'm about to ask you to do something important for me."

His grandfather paused before continuing.

"When you were three and a half years old, you and your father were in a serious traffic accident. Your spine was damaged – crushed, I suppose is the right word. I was at a dig in Tibet when it happened. I dropped everything and caught the first flight back to London. Your father was in a coma with a broken neck, and you… There wasn't anything the doctors could do, just give you morphine and wait while nature took

175

its course. I had to do something – I had no choice. There was only one thing that could save you."

His grandfather paused again.

"I knew the Institute would never let me have it. Never let it be removed from the vault. Not even for me, or my grandson. So I was left with only one option: I had to steal it. After I gave you the luridium, you got better. But the Institute came after me. Abraham Talley, too. I was under attack from all sides. I had stolen the only luridium we'd managed to find. I had to get away. Draw the attention away from you."

His grandfather adjusted his glasses.

"I knew that by giving you the luridium I would be creating what the Institute and I had been working so hard to prevent. Luridium spreading to people, and finally...

"When luridium gets into a person's system, it takes over the injured parts of the body. In your case, this was the spine and parts of your brain. Even before the accident I could tell that you had a special knack for codebreaking. Once you had the luridium in you, I knew this talent would be multiplied a hundredfold. That makes you the very best cryptographer in the world, William. So you have to be careful. There are a lot of people who will want to use you. Without the luridium you wouldn't have survived, but you're not quite as human as you thought you were... You're forty-nine per cent luridium, William."

Everything went black before William's eyes. His legs

felt like jelly, and he fell to his knees. He couldn't believe it. Could he really have luridium inside him? He looked at his hands. Besides them shaking in shock, they seemed completely normal. His head was exploding with questions. He looked up at his grandfather.

"I know it's a lot to process, William," his grandfather continued. "You have to give it time, and let it sink in."

"But – but how?" William stuttered. He was still dazed from the shock. "How can I be full of luridium? I still feel like … myself."

William knew he was talking to a hologram, and that he wouldn't get a reply. But he had to say it out loud, for his own sake.

The hologram didn't say anything more for a while. It was as if his grandfather wanted to give William some time to process this information. Think things over.

Then the old man smiled and spoke again. "I bet you're bursting with questions. But that will have to wait. There are more urgent matters at hand."

William knew that his grandfather was right. It was no use asking questions now. He had to concentrate. He sensed that there was more important information coming.

"All this means that you're different from everyone else," the hologram continued. "You have a special talent. For codes."

His grandfather fell silent again. He removed his glasses and cleaned them with his shirt sleeve. Then put them back on.

"Abraham wants to get his hands on the luridium that's inside you, William. And if he finds you..." His grandfather stopped. As if even the thought of what would happen was paralysing to him.

"The most important thing for you to do now is to find me. My body is cryogenically frozen in a secret bunker in the tunnels deep beneath Victoria Station," continued the hologram, blinking a little as if it was losing power. William moved closer.

"It's important that you come alone. I don't think you can trust the others. Use your powers to find me. You have to let go of yourself and let the luridium inside you be your guide. And bring your orb. You won't be able to get in without it."

The hologram hissed and blinked again.

"Find the cryogenic chamber behind the large metal door. You'll need to decipher the locks to get in. But I suspect that you're the one person, besides me, who can do it. There are ten cryogenic tanks down there. It's important that you only thaw Number Seven." His grandfather paused once more and looked serious. "Number Seven," he repeated as if to make sure it had really sunk in.

The lights in the room blinked. The hologram of his grandfather quivered a couple of times and then disappeared with a *zap*.

"Grandfather?" William said, but there was no response.

William stood, dazed, in the middle of the room. Was this

really true? Was he forty-nine per cent intelligent metal? In other words, a kind of machine?

He touched his face with a trembling hand. He felt the same as before, human. He needed air.

He had to get out. His eyes turned to the red emergency hatch in the wall.

CHAPTER 32

William hit the snow face first. He lay gasping for breath. He didn't know how long he'd been running or how far he'd come. After he'd made it out of the Centre for Misinformation, he'd hardly looked back. The emergency hatch had shot him out onto a dark back street. From there he had just run.

It had been snowing hard for the last hour, and there wasn't much warmth in his thin tweed jacket. His only company up until this point had been snowploughs and taxis, but by now the streets were full of people.

When he finally caught his breath, he sat up. He was in a large park. Busy people scurried by.

Suddenly he heard someone behind him call, "William!"

He recognized the voice and turned around.

"Iscia?" he whispered.

Iscia helped him up and began to tug him along. "Come on," she whispered.

A while later, William and Iscia were sitting in a small

café. Pleasant piano music streamed out of a speaker in the ceiling. The café was half full of people queuing to buy their morning coffee. William and Iscia sat in a quiet corner by the window. Iscia kept glancing out of it, as if she was waiting for someone. Or was scared.

William rubbed his hands on his thighs and felt as if he was starting to get the feeling back in his fingers. A smiling woman came over to them.

"What can I get for you?" she asked.

"Uh." William cleared his throat. "I don't have any—"

"I have money," Iscia said, looking up at the waitress. "Could we have two large pancakes with whipped cream and two cups of hot chocolate? Also with whipped cream?"

The woman jotted their order down on her notepad and left again.

They sat in silence for a while. William looked around. Everything seemed so normal.

"What are you doing here?" he asked.

"I ran away," she said, sounding a little nervous.

"Why?"

"I'd rather not talk about it."

"How did you find me?"

"It wasn't that hard, actually," Iscia said. "Taking the vacuum train to the Centre for Misinformation is standard procedure when the Institute is under attack."

William hesitated. It seemed too simple. She had found him

too easily. Could he really trust her? He needed to know more.

"Is the Institute attacked often?" William asked.

"No," she said. "At least never while I've been there."

"So how do you know about the vacuum train?"

"I've read the rules," she said, smiling slyly. "Don't you trust me?"

William didn't answer, just stared at her. He could see her squirming a bit now. As if she was searching for something to say.

"When you, Goffman and Slapperton all suddenly disappeared after the attack," she continued, "I figured you'd escaped by vacuum train to London. I decided to follow you."

William decided to let his suspicions rest for a while. He was glad she was here.

"How's everyone else? Was anyone injured?" William asked.

"Whatever attacked disappeared right afterwards," she said. "It seems as if it was only interested in you guys. Do you have any idea why?"

William shook his head and looked down at the café table.

"Are you all right?" she asked, her voice sounding worried.

"Yeah," William said without meeting her gaze.

He was dying to tell her everything, that he was part metal, like a machine. He needed to share it with someone, but he couldn't. His grandfather had told him not to tell anyone.

Besides, he wasn't sure how Iscia would respond.

He looked up at her. He suddenly thought about her strange reaction when she found her folder. That was the last time he had seen her.

"Can I ask you something?" he said.

"What?" she replied.

"You remember back at the Institute – when you found your folder?"

She stopped smiling. As if she was suddenly reminded of something bad.

"Why did you react like that?"

She busied herself scraping at a small crack in the table with her fingernail.

"I'd rather not talk about it," she whispered. "Do you mind?"

"OK," he said. "But—"

He was interrupted by the waitress returning with steaming hot pancakes and two large mugs of hot chocolate. She smiled at them as she set their order down.

"Enjoy!" she said and left.

William was glad the food was here. He was starving and the conversation had got much too serious. He took a bite and closed his eyes. For a brief second he dreamed he was far away. It was like being at home again. His mother always made pancakes for breakfast on Sundays. He took a gulp of the cocoa, and felt the warmth spread through his body. He opened his eyes, looked at Iscia and smiled. She smiled back.

"Why are you alone? Where are the others?" she asked, taking a bite of her pancake.

William hesitated. He didn't really know what to say. Could he trust her? He remembered that after her strange behaviour when she'd found her folder, Goffman had wanted to talk to her. But if he couldn't trust her, who could he trust? He decided to tell her some of the truth.

"I ran away. Just like you," he said, smiling apologetically.

"You ran away? Why?" she exclaimed. "Does this have something to do with your grandfather? Did you find anything in his folder in the Archive?"

"Yeah, it has something to do with him," William said, hesitating. "Someone is after me."

"Who?"

"I can't say much, Iscia. Maybe I can tell you more later. After things have calmed down."

"But what's your plan? Are you going to run around London alone?" she asked.

"I have to find my grandfather. He's—"

William stopped short when he caught sight of an old woman standing on the pavement outside. He recognized her right away. It was the old woman from the Institute. Or, as he now knew, the two drivers.

"We have to go," he said, pulling Iscia with him. "They've found us."

CHAPTER 33

After running for what seemed like for ever, William and Iscia finally stopped outside the main entrance to Victoria Station. William wiped the sweat off his face and looked around them.

"There she is," Iscia whispered, pointing across the street.

Sure enough, the old woman was pushing her way through the crowd on the pavement. She walked right out into the road, her eyes trained on William. A bus had to slam on its brakes to avoid hitting her, but she carried on crossing as if nothing had happened.

"Come on," William said, pulling Iscia along.

They scrambled down the steps into Victoria Underground Station and were soon swallowed up by the throng of people on the concourse. They stopped in front of a row of automatic ticket barriers.

"How do we get through?" William asked, looking behind him nervously.

"Watch this," Iscia said, following an overweight man in a suit to one of the ticket barriers. He pressed his Oyster Card against the electronic reader and she slipped in after him before the barriers closed.

"Look out!" she called, pointing to the old woman, who was coming down the stairs behind William.

William took a run-up and leaped over one of the gates that was meant for wheelchair users and buggies. A deep male voice rang out behind him: "Hey, you!"

William turned and saw that a station guard had seen him.

"Run, William!" Iscia cried.

She raced towards the escalators that led deeper underground. William followed.

The escalators were crowded, and seemed to be creeping downwards at a snail's pace. William looked back. The guard was gone, but the old woman was right behind him, pushing people out of her way with her cane and drawing dangerously close.

"This way!" William called, climbing up onto the raised central area between the two escalators. He sat with his legs out in front of him and slid down. Iscia did the same. Fast.

A little too fast.

William landed first, crashing into a man who was standing at the bottom of the escalators playing his violin. They both fell to the ground. The violin slid across the floor.

"Sorry, sorry!" said William as he pulled himself to his feet.

The violinist got up, dazed, and looked around for his violin.

"Watch out!" cried Iscia as she careened towards them.

William hurriedly picked up the violin and handed it to the violinist.

"Sorry," William said again, before he and Iscia vanished into the crowd on the platform.

"Get down!" William hissed.

Soon he and Iscia were crawling on all fours along the filthy platform. Then William stopped.

"Listen," he said.

It was the sound of a tube train approaching. They stood up cautiously and hurried towards the far end of the platform.

Suddenly William spotted something – something small and shiny – and it was moving. He stopped and looked around, but it was gone. Was he seeing things? No, there it was again. It darted between the legs of the people ahead of him and then it was gone.

"What is it?" asked Iscia.

"I thought I saw something..." he began, but broke off when he spotted a creature peeking out from behind a briefcase sitting on the platform a short way away. "The *beetle*?" William exclaimed.

The little beetle zigzagged towards them.

"What is *that*?" Iscia whispered.

"That's the beetle that came to my room at home right before my family was attacked," William said.

"Attacked?" Iscia repeated.

William watched as the beetle hopped up and down, then turned and rushed towards the edge of the platform.

"It got me out of the house," he said. "Maybe it's trying to help us now?"

The train thundered into the station, the doors opened and people poured out. The beetle buzzed onto the train and vanished amongst all the feet.

"We have to get on it," William said.

He and Iscia pushed their way into the end carriage. William cast a glance back and spotted the old woman elbowing her way into the same carriage. The doors closed and the train started moving.

William squatted down next to Iscia.

"She got on. She's in here," he whispered.

"What do we do now?" Iscia whispered back.

The little beetle hovered in front of them, bouncing around as if awaiting instructions. William cautiously stood up. The old woman was standing over by the door, narrow eyes slowly scanning the crowd. William ducked back down.

"We have to get out of here," he whispered. "She's by the doors. When people get off at the next station, we'll have nowhere to hide."

"But how can we get off if she's blocking the doors?" Iscia whispered.

William thought this over. Then he had an idea. "Follow

me. We don't have any choice. This is our only option."

William opened the door to the empty driver's compartment at the end of the carriage, and Iscia followed. A door beyond led out of the very back of the train. The little beetle fidgeted around eagerly beside them.

"Are you insane?" Iscia exclaimed. "We're going to jump off a train travelling at full speed?"

"Do you have a better idea?"

William slid the last door open and they peered down at the tracks flashing by. There was a space between the central electric rails. The beetle crawled up his trouser leg and hid in the inside pocket of his tweed jacket.

"Come on. On the count of three," William said, taking Iscia's hand. "One ... two ... three..."

They jumped together, keeping straight so they landed in the gap between the middle rails.

"Whoa!" William exhaled as he got to his feet, checking he was still in one piece. "That's what I call an emergency exit."

"Well, I don't *think* I got electrocuted," Iscia said, testing her fingers for sparks.

"I think we got away," William said shakily as the train disappeared into the darkness.

"I really hope so," said Iscia. "What do we do now?"

William scanned the tunnel.

Small soot-covered lamps were attached to the walls, and gave off just enough light that they could more or less make out their surroundings. Something dripped from the ceiling, and the air smelled dank, musty and old.

Suddenly Iscia grabbed William's arm, her eyes wide with fear.

"William," she whispered, her voice trembling as she pointed in the direction the train had gone.

William turned to see the old woman walking towards them.

CHAPTER 34

"Come on, she hasn't seen us yet!" William whispered, pulling Iscia along in the opposite direction. The pair ran.

Eventually William called out for them to stop. He looked around the dark tunnel. Aside from a dirty light on the wall in front of them, everything was dark. They were both dripping in sweat. Iscia bent over double next to him, trying to catch her breath. In the dim light she saw something move, and edged away. William jumped back as a fat rat darted across the tracks and vanished into a crack in the wall.

"I hate rats," she said drily.

William was about to set off again when he heard a sound.

Iscia had heard it too. "What is that rumbling?"

A cool draught of air came out of the darkness towards them. The rumbling increased. William could feel the vibrations in the ground now.

"Train," he said quietly, looking around for somewhere to seek refuge.

"It's going to crush us!" Iscia exclaimed, pointing at two glowing dots that were approaching menacingly.

The tunnel floor was really shaking now. Panic rose in William, but he tried to push it back down.

"We have to get away from it!" Iscia grabbed his arm.

"Where?" William shouted over the roar from the oncoming train. He could see the front of it clearly now. It was barely thirty metres away.

"Up against the wall?" she shouted.

"There's not enough room," William said. "It'll hit us."

"Quick!" Iscia yelled.

They started running again, but the mix of gravel and train tracks made it almost impossible. The train drew closer with every step.

"Wave at the driver!" Iscia called. "Maybe he'll be able to stop!"

"Not enough time!" William shouted back.

"Then we're about to be mincemeat!" William could see the fear in Iscia's eyes now.

Then something occurred to him: the orb! He still had it in his jacket pocket. It was a long shot. But the only shot he had. He pulled out the orb and turned it as he ran. Suddenly the display blinked to life and showed a number four. The level he had reached during the duel with Freddy.

"What are you doing?" yelled Iscia.

William hurled the orb over his shoulder as he ran. Turning

back, he watched it bounce softly in mid-air. Then a blue beam of light shot out, forming a wall just like the one that had saved him from Freddy's orb. The train hit the wall, pushing the orb in front of it.

"It's slowing down!" Iscia cried.

William watched as the train slowed and eventually came to a complete halt.

"You did it!" Iscia cried. "Get the orb. They're coming out." She pointed up at the train, where the silhouettes of the passengers on board could just about be seen through the windows. "If they catch us we're in big trouble."

William grabbed the orb and the light wall disappeared, just as a train door slid open and a man in uniform appeared in the opening.

"HEY!" the man shouted.

William and Iscia couldn't run any more. William stood panting like a wild animal. His lungs felt as if they were going to explode.

"Now what?" Iscia asked.

"Well, we can't keep wandering around in these tunnels," William said. "There are only so many full-speed trains we can dodge. He said the orb would lead the way," he muttered to himself.

"Who?" Iscia asked.

"My grandfather…"

"You talked to him?"

"Yes. Well, in a way," William said, and then turned to face her. "It was a hologram. It appeared last night." He hesitated. "My grandfather is down here somewhere, frozen. I have to set him free."

"Frozen?" Iscia exclaimed.

"Yeah."

William pulled his orb out of his pocket. Iscia stumbled to her feet and stared down the dark tunnel.

"You don't have to come with me if you don't want to. It'll be dangerous," William said, looking at her again.

"I don't have anything better do," she replied. "Besides, I don't really want to go back and run into that woman again. Or another train."

"I have to get this working," William said, closing his eyes and focusing on his orb.

"You're doing that now? Here?" he heard Iscia say.

He waited.

Nothing happened.

William concentrated. He had to do this. He had to get to the next level. Had to trust his instincts.

"Come on," Iscia said. "I think I can hear another train."

"You're not exactly helping," William said crossly. "Let me concentrate."

And then came that familiar feeling, spreading out from his stomach like a faint ache below his belly button. The vibrations grew stronger and stronger, moving up his spine and out into his hands. His fingers started working. *Click ... click ... click.*

When William opened his eyes he could see all the different symbols from the orb floating in front of him. Some were glowing brightly, others had faded to the background. He looked down at his hands. They moved quickly. Faster and faster. Now the only sound he could hear was the clicking from the orb.

Click ... click ... click ... click.

Then his hands suddenly stopped and the symbols floated back towards the orb again and gently settled on its surface.

The orb rose up out of his hands. William opened his eyes. It hovered in the air in front of him and twisted from side to side, orienting itself. A blue beam shot out of it, and quickly moved over the walls and ceiling. When the beam disappeared, the orb began to fly away down the tunnel. It didn't look as if it was planning to wait for them.

"Come on," William called, following it.

The orb led them through what felt like an interminable labyrinth of old, disused tunnels, rounded a corner and paused.

William froze, staring ahead of them. Iscia stopped beside him.

"It tricked us!" She was angry.

There was nothing but a dirty brick wall in front of them.

"No! Look! It wants us to keep going," William said.

The orb kept moving, slowly, straight ahead, stopping when it bumped into the wall.

Thud … thud … thud. It was as if the orb was trying to get through the wall.

"I don't think it tricked us," William said, placing his hand on the rough surface of the wall. "This is old," he added.

He remembered what Goffman had said about the sealed-up tunnel. "It's here. I just know it is." William took a couple of steps back.

If his grandfather had found this wall, he must have got through it somehow.

"Why right here? Why this one? We've already passed a ton of walls just like this," Iscia said. She felt the surface as she'd seen William do. "Do you really think there's a secret door here somewhere?"

William peered down at the ground below, where the orb was hovering, and spotted something sticking up out of the gravel. It looked like a handle made of steel. He squatted down and began to dig.

"Look here, I've found something!" he exclaimed. Iscia knelt down next to him to help.

"It's some kind of lid," William said, once he'd removed all the gravel. He ran his hand over what appeared to be a man-hole cover.

"Are we going down into the sewer?" Iscia said, wrinkling her nose.

"I don't think this is a sewer. It doesn't look that old. Maybe this is how my grandfather got in, by digging," William said, trying to lift the lid. It wouldn't budge. "Help me!"

They both pulled with all their might, but it was stuck.

"What is it?" Iscia asked, noticing that something had grabbed William's attention.

"Look at that!" he said, pointing to a line of symbols on the lid.

William recognized the symbols right away. He'd seen them before. Many times. He put his hand into his pocket and pulled out the old picture of his grandfather's desk.

"Of course," he said, brushing the sand away from the steel frame surrounding the lid. A thin line came into view. "We don't lift it. We *twist* it. The whole lid is a kind of combination lock. Let's give it a go."

William looked again at the photograph, studying the order of the symbols that were carved into the desk. He hoped he was right. They didn't have time to lose.

"To the left," he said, stuffing the photo back in his pocket and grabbing the handle.

Iscia did the same. They pulled. The lid moved surprisingly easily now, as if it was on ball bearings. When the first symbol hit the mark, the massive lock emitted a clang from deep within.

They twisted the lid back and forth through the whole set of symbols. It was getting increasingly harder to move. There was only one turn left. William pulled on the lid. It was so hard to move now, and his hands were so exhausted, he thought he wouldn't make it.

"Look!" Iscia cried, pointing into the darkness.

William looked up and his heart almost stopped.

A figure was coming towards them through the dark. The old woman. But she wasn't moving like an old woman any more. She raced like a sprinter over the tracks, lightning fast.

"Come on!" William cried.

He pulled on the lid with all his might. Together, he and Iscia managed to move it a fraction. But not enough to reach the last symbol. William looked towards the old woman. She was about fifty metres away now. Suddenly she split in two as she ran, transforming once more into the two drivers.

William gathered all his remaining strength. Focusing on his grandfather and how close he was to finally finding him, he felt a burst of adrenaline shoot through his veins and he pulled as if his life depended on it.

There was a faint creak from the lid … and it flipped up in a cloud of dust. A rusty metal ladder disappeared down into darkness.

William grabbed hold of Iscia and pulled her towards the hole.

"Get in!" he shouted.

Iscia jumped in. The beetle suddenly shot out from William's pocket and followed her down the hole.

William grabbed the hovering orb and cast a last glance at the drivers, who lunged for him through the air like a pair of attacking tigers.

William threw himself down into the dark hole, pulling the lid closed after him.

CHAPTER 35

"Iscia?" William whispered.

The darkness was impenetrable. All he could hear was the sound of the drivers banging on the massive lid above them.

They wouldn't be able to solve the code, William thought. But they probably had some kind of weapon or device to get through the entrance now that William had located it. William knew they had to hurry.

"Iscia?" he whispered again. Again nothing.

William stepped into the darkness. Gravel and sand crunched beneath his shoes. His hand felt a stone wall and followed it until he came to another wall, blocking his way. He felt panic rising. He had never liked confined spaces. He started breathing faster. The air down here was even worse than in the tube tunnels.

"Where are you, Iscia?" he tried again, louder this time.

"Up here," he heard from somewhere above him. "There's a ladder!"

William groped around until he found rungs leading upwards. He began to climb.

Iscia was standing by a natural rock wall, running her hand over the surface of the stone. The little beetle was rubbing itself affectionately against her leg.

"Isn't it beautiful?" she said dreamily, looking at the wall.

William stared at the faint blue light emanating from the rock face. He'd seen that light before. Inside the container Slapperton had shown him in the cellar at the Institute. His whole body started trembling. It couldn't be far to his grandfather now.

"Look at that," Iscia said, pointing to a wire hanging from the ceiling.

"Is that a lamp?" William moved closer. The blue gleam from the rock face gave off just enough light for him to make out their surroundings.

"Maybe there's a switch somewhere?" Iscia said.

William looked around them. In the distance he could hear the drivers pounding on the lid.

"I don't think we have much time…" he said.

"Bingo!" Iscia exclaimed. She flipped the switch and a single bulb came on.

William shuddered.

They were standing in the middle of an unfinished tunnel. Old wooden beams lay around, and a few rusty pickaxes were leaning against the stone wall. The end of the tunnel had collapsed in a pile of rubble.

"It's here," William whispered.

"What is this?" Iscia asked.

She'd stopped by a large, dust-covered brass plate that was bolted to the side of the rock face. William wiped the dust off the plate. A chill ran down his spine as he read the words: *In memory of those who perished.*

"Is this where those men died?" Iscia whispered.

"Yes," William said.

"This is creepy," she said, shrinking back.

But where was the door? There was nothing here but rubble. William turned his attention back to the brass plate. Why did it need to be so big for just a few words?

William reached up to the edge of the plate. He felt a cold draught of air. There had to be an opening behind it. He worked a couple of his fingers in and pulled. The rusty screws that held the plate in place soon gave way and it fell to the ground with a *clank.*

In the wall behind was a round metal hole. It looked like the end of some kind of concrete pipe and was just big enough for a grown man to crawl through.

Suddenly something moved inside the pipe. William pulled back as a black rat stuck its head out of the end and sniffed at them. Iscia picked up a small stone and threw it at the rat, which squeaked and backed into the darkness again.

"I really, really hate rats," Iscia said, shuddering.

"Me too," said William. "But I think that's where we have

to go. I can feel it." He put a hand on his stomach. He could feel a slight tremor. That was usually a sign that he was close to some kind of code.

"I'll go first," Iscia offered.

William looked at her. He could see the fear in her eyes. She really didn't want to go in there.

"No, I'll go," William said. "It's *my* grandfather we're looking for, remember. Besides … you *really* hate rats." He swallowed, forced a smiled and looked at the pipe.

"OK," Iscia said. "I'll be right behind you."

William bent forward and felt around inside the dark pipe. It felt moist and slimy. He wanted to pull back, but the tremors had increased in strength. He must be on the right track.

Soon William was crawling through the pipe. He could see nothing in front of him but darkness. And the smell was almost unbearable. It took all of his concentration not to give in to claustrophobia. He could hear Iscia breathing behind him. It felt good to have her close.

William stopped as he caught a glimpse of a patch of light up ahead.

"There it is," he whispered.

He started crawling again. Faster and faster.

They were so close. They had to get out.

CHAPTER 36

William and Iscia stared around them in awe. Neither said a word.

They were in a vast cave. The rock walls pulsed with strong blue light. It was the most beautiful thing William had ever seen. A gigantic iron door towered in the middle of the cave wall. A pile of empty wooden crates stood beside the door, each with *Dynamite* written on the side. From the last attempt to blast through, William realized.

The little beetle moved restlessly between the two children, its metal feet tapping on the stone floor.

"Wh-what is that?" Iscia stammered.

"The door," William whispered.

He approached cautiously.

The door was covered with symbols. These were the symbols his grandfather had managed to decipher. These were the symbols that had told him about luridium and how dangerous it could be.

This was where Abraham Talley had found the first clump of the intelligent metal over a hundred and fifty years ago. And maybe this was where his grandfather was now.

William held out his orb. "Show me what to do," he whispered.

He closed his eyes and tried to invoke the vibrations. Nothing happened.

"Come on, come on," he muttered.

"What are you waiting for?" he heard Iscia say.

"I'm trying," he said through gritted teeth. "I'm trying."

He began to panic. Had he lost his gift, right when he needed it most?

William didn't know if it was because he was completely exhausted or because he'd just found out he was not who he had always thought he was, but suddenly he felt utterly powerless. How had he ever got himself into this? He only had himself to blame. Why couldn't he have just kept his fingers off the Impossible Puzzle that day in the museum? Then everything could have stayed as it was. He should have listened to his parents. He would still be sitting in his room working on deciphering some harmless code or other. His father had been completely right: he should have stayed well away from codes. But now it was way too late. Nothing could ever be the same again.

The only thing that kept him going now was the fact that he was closer to finding his grandfather than he had ever been.

He had to go on. When he found Tobias, everything would be OK again.

And then suddenly it was as if he knew what he had to do. He had to accept what he was. There was no going back.

I am intelligent metal … I am intelligent metal, he repeated to himself. *I am just fifty-one per cent human.*

"They're coming through the wall," he heard Iscia say from somewhere far away.

But William couldn't speak. He couldn't even open his eyes. He felt that familiar ache in his stomach. It grew and became much stronger than usual. Soon his whole spine was quivering. It felt as if his body was going to shake apart. The vibrations spread through his arms to his hands, and his fingers started working crazily. The inside of the orb clicked and clicked.

When he opened his eyes he couldn't believe what he saw. The symbols on the door were pulsating with a golden light. Some of the symbols rose up off the surface and hovered, coming towards him. They formed new patterns, many of which he now recognized. Some he had seen on his grandfather's desk, while others were engraved in the orb. His fingers worked faster and faster. It was as if he understood what the symbols meant now, as if he could suddenly read an ancient language. Even though he couldn't explain it, he now understood what luridium was and how it could be used for good or evil. He understood why Abraham was so desperate for more, and what kind of strength lay hidden deep within his own body. It was both amazing and frightening at the same time.

The vibrations receded and his fingers stopped their frenetic work. The orb floated up from his hands, glided over to the middle of the door and then vanished into a hole.

"You did it!" he heard Iscia cheer behind him.

A rumbling came from deep inside the door. William took a step back, and watched as it slowly slid open.

CHAPTER 37

The next moments were like a dream for William, hazy images and sounds that seemed far away. Blue light. Iscia yelling. The heavy door closing behind them.

"William? William! Can you hear me, William?"

Mostly he wanted to sleep. He was so unbelievably tired, he needed to rest. It felt as if that last puzzle had broken him.

"You have to wake up!" Iscia cried.

Slowly his hearing returned and objects seemed to come back into focus. His thoughts cleared.

"I-I'm fine," he stammered, but he was still dizzy. "Where are we?"

"I don't know," Iscia said, standing up. "What kind of place is this?"

"Where are the drivers?" William asked.

"They're on the other side of that," she said, pointing to the large iron door. "They were just about to reach us when the door closed."

William got to his feet. His orb was hovering in the air beside him.

"It worked," he said to himself. Then he thought of something. "Did you see what happened to the beetle?"

"Yeah. It went that way," Iscia said, pointing.

William turned to follow her finger and gasped.

Before them, an enormous chamber stretched into the distance, and it was filled with row upon row of huge submarines. Here and there, water drops fell from the carved stone ceiling high above.

"Wowww!" he exclaimed.

His eyes travelled over the silent metal giants. Too many to count. Suddenly he felt tiny and insignificant.

Behind the submarines stood line after line of trucks, tanks and military motorcycles, which seemed to stretch endlessly into the gigantic hall.

"What is this? Some kind of military depot?" Iscia asked.

"Looks like it's from the Second World War," William said, taking a couple of shaky steps forward.

"Do you think anyone knows about this?" she asked.

"The Institute knows about it," William said. "And Abraham Talley, I bet. But I don't think any of them have actually managed to get in here… So why in the world is the ancient technology chamber full of equipment from the War?"

William stood for a moment, thinking. Had Goffman and Slapperton been lying to him? Or did they not know about this?

"But why store submarines down here? There isn't even any water," Iscia said.

"I have no idea," William said, going up to one of the submarines and knocking on the metal with his fist.

"Do you think we're safe here?" Iscia asked, glancing back at the huge door behind them.

"As long as we don't open it for them," William said, pointing to a lever on the wall. "It looks like it can only be opened from the inside. I just hope there's nothing in here we need to worry about. Come on."

They continued towards the rows of military trucks.

"Is he in here somewhere, do you think? Your grandfather?" Iscia asked. "That's what he said, wasn't it? We just have to find out where he is."

They stopped in front of a red steel door. The sign said: *Cryogenic Lab.*

"It must be in here," murmured Iscia.

William put his hand on the handle. "It's locked."

He looked around and spotted a military tank parked a short way off. He headed towards it.

"Um, have you ever driven something like that before?" Iscia asked.

"There has to be a first time for everything," he replied casually.

Inside the tank, William ran his fingers over the instrument panel. His forefinger stopped at one of the buttons.

"Sometimes you just have to trust your gut," he said and pressed it.

Iscia yelped as her seatback suddenly released and she found herself reclining all the way back.

"Sorry," William said, trying another button. The whole tank shook as its powerful motor began to rumble.

William pulled on both control levers and put his foot on the pedal. The tank jumped.

"Careful," Iscia said, grabbing her seat firmly as William turned and twisted the stick to the side. The tank turned to aim its gun turret at the red door. Suddenly they heard a loud explosion.

Then all went quiet. William opened the hatch in the roof and they both peered out. William's eyes widened. "Wow."

Iscia smiled. The red metal door had gone. A dark, smoke-filled crater gaped back at them where it had been.

CHAPTER 38

"This is it!" William cried.

Iscia followed him.

Ten enormous containers stood in a row in front of them. The containers reached all the way up to the ceiling, and were numbered from one to ten.

"Who on earth could have made these?" she asked.

"I don't know," William said. His voice was filled with awe.

"What do you reckon's inside?"

"I don't want to find out." William's eyes scanned the containers and stopped at one of them. "I just want to find the one with my grandfather in it, and get him out."

He walked over to Container Number Seven and wiped the dust off a small instrument panel.

"Minus one hundred and ninety-six centigrade," he read.

"What does this mean?" Iscia asked, pointing to the control panel on one of the other containers. A red light was blinking ominously. William went over to look.

"This one is at minus ninety-eight. And it's rising all the time," he said, glancing at Iscia with concern. "It looks like it's thawing."

He looked at the display again: now minus fifty-eight degrees. They could hear rumbling and gurgling from inside.

"This one's also dropping." Iscia pointed at the meter on another container.

"What's going on?" William gasped.

"They're all thawing," Iscia said with dread in her voice. "There's no way this is safe." She took a step back.

"It depends what's inside," William said. They stood staring at the temperature gauges, which were rapidly rising.

"It's happening to all of them. Maybe the explosion triggered it," Iscia said.

The meter on the first tank hit the zero mark. Everything went quiet, then the container split in two. Grey mist rose out. William and Iscia drew back and watched the cold clouds billow towards them like a sleepy flood.

"I have a bad feeling about this…" Iscia said.

So did William. He raised a trembling hand and pointed at something in front of them. Something moving inside the smoke. Something big.

"RUN!" he yelled, yanking Iscia along behind him.

They jumped back through the hole in the wall, heading for the tank they had used to blow open the door.

The wall behind them exploded into a cloud of dust and pieces of rubble and concrete.

The dust cleared to reveal an enormous robot standing where the wall had been. Mounted on the top of its body was the head of a wild boar, with glowing red eyes and long tusks. When the boar-bot spotted William and Iscia, who had now reached the tank, it emitted a deafening howl and stomped towards them, causing the floor to shake.

"It's all over," William whispered.

"Look, there!" Iscia cried, pointing.

The little beetle scurried past them towards the boar-bot, which stopped abruptly when it spotted the small creature.

The beetle suddenly began to vibrate intensely.

"What is it doing?" Iscia asked, scared.

"No idea," said William.

The boar-bot stood watching the tiny beetle, which was now vibrating so violently it seemed to have trouble running. A series of loud *clacks* came from the beetle as it continued towards the boar. Then it started to unfold itself somehow. Metal plate upon metal plate seemed to appear from within its body. And it was growing bigger.

"It's shape-shifting," Iscia whispered.

William stood, transfixed, staring at the little beetle's dramatic transformation.

The boar-bot took a step back as it, too, stared at the creature that was heading towards it. It was no longer a beetle, every clack and every mechanical change making it more and more humanoid. It now looked like a huge upright robot with the head of a beetle. Long metal antlers pierced the air as it picked up speed and headed straight for the boar-bot.

"It's going to attack the boar-bot..." William said. The ground under his feet vibrated for every step the enormous beetle-bot took. The clacking grew louder as it picked up speed.

The boar-bot pulled back and picked up one of the tanks. It flung it at the giant beetle-bot, which batted the tank away as if it weighed no more than a football. The beetle-bot then stretched out a leg and tripped the boar-bot, which hit the ground with a devastating thump. The beetle-bot stopped. The dry clacking slowed down.

Clack ... clack ... clack...

"It saved us!" Iscia cheered.

But William wasn't cheering. He was thinking about how the beetle had been there just before his house was attacked. At the time he had wondered if it had come to help him escape, but...

"What is it?" Iscia asked when she saw William's expression. The beetle-bot turned and looked at them.

"I don't think it's over," William whispered, backing away. "That's the one."

"What one?" Iscia asked.

"Abraham's robot. *The beetle is his robot*," William

whispered, crawling up onto the tank. He held out his hand to Iscia and pulled her after him.

"What robot?" Iscia asked.

"The one that attacked us in Norway," William whispered.

The beetle-bot was now bounding across the hall towards then in long strides, flinging aside military trucks and tanks as if they were made of paper.

The hatch in the roof of the tank was still ajar and William grasped it with both hands, pulling with all his strength. The hatch swung open and William grabbed Iscia's arm.

"GET IN!" he shouted. "IT'S NOT GOING TO STOP!"

Iscia jumped through the hatch, William following close behind, and they just managed to pull it shut before the beetle-bot hit the tank with such force that it lifted the vehicle right off the ground. Inside, Iscia screamed and flailed around for something to hold on to. The pair crashed to the floor and lay there, stunned.

William's ears were ringing. He'd hit his head hard in the collision. He sat up and looked out of the window. The beetle-bot was heading back towards them.

"It's coming in for another attack!" he cried, clinging to the seat.

They felt the tank being lifted up. It crashed into a wall and then hit the floor with a loud clang.

"Iscia?" William called out.

She was underneath one of the seats. He crawled over and

shook her. "Iscia? Iscia!" he cried, cautiously rolling her over onto her back.

She didn't respond.

He slid away as the tank was lifted again but clambered back and flung himself over Iscia to protect her from the new assault. Only it didn't come. William opened his eyes and looked around. He jumped when he saw two glowing eyes glaring in at him through one of the windows.

William crawled over to the other window and peered out. The tank was swaying in the beetle-bot's hand, high above the ground. William knew they wouldn't survive another smashing. He had to do something.

He grabbed the control lever and yanked it to one side. The tank's turret spun around until it was pointing right at the giant robot body. William felt the tank jerk as it was hoisted even higher. The robot was getting ready to throw them again.

William clung to the control panel and hit the fire button. A loud *boom* echoed all around them. The beetle-bot staggered back and forth, and finally fell over backwards. The tank dropped to the floor, and then ... complete silence.

William lay there, listening. He cautiously peered through the window again but couldn't see anything.

"Iscia!" he called, crawling over to her. He put his ear to her lips. Was she breathing? "Iscia, can you hear me?"

No response.

"ISCIA!"

CHAPTER 39

"I think my leg is broken," Iscia moaned.

She was lying next to one of the submarines on an old mattress. Gently, William placed his folded jacket under her head.

The beetle-bot lay lifeless a short distance away, the tank on top of it.

"Are there more of them coming?" Iscia asked, squinting at the robot.

"I don't know," William said. "I've only ever seen one beetle. I think."

"What about that thing?" Iscia said, pointing at what was left of the boar-bot.

"There might be more of them inside the other containers," William said with a shudder.

"Get your grandfather out of there before any of the others thaw out, then," Iscia said. "I'll wait here."

"Are you sure?" William asked.

"Yes, I'll yell if I need help," she said, smiling as bravely as she could. "It doesn't sound like any of the other containers have finished thawing yet."

"Maybe there was only one of them," William said.

"Let's hope so." Iscia winced in pain and clutched at her leg.

"I'll be back as soon as I can," William said and hurried back towards the cryogenic chamber.

He stopped in front of the large containers and checked the displays. The temperatures inside were still dropping – some faster than others. He found Container Number Seven and looked at the thermometer. The display showed thirty-seven degrees.

He stood for a few seconds, unsure what to do. Part of him just wanted to run and get out of there. Who knew what could emerge from the other containers? But this was his only chance of seeing his grandfather again. He had to stay.

By the time he noticed an enormous shape emerging from one of the other containers, it was already too late. He looked up to see another robot looming over him. The robot whacked him on the head with a large metallic hand, then everything went black.

What's going on? Where am I?

William sat up cautiously.

His head felt as if it was about to explode, and he was wet and cold.

"William?" a voice said. "William, you have to wake up."

"Grandpa?"

William blinked. There was a blurred figure crouching in front of him.

"Careful," the voice said. "You suffered a bit of a bump."

William put his hands to his head. "Grandpa?" he repeated.

"Here, give me your hand."

William lifted his arm. He felt someone take his hand and help him up to a sitting position.

"There, like that. Very good, now lean back carefully."

William leaned back and discovered there was a wall behind him. He began to make out more details of the figure before him. Two friendly eyes, shaggy grey hair, a beard.

"Grandpa?"

"Yes, it's me," his grandfather said.

Before William knew it, his arms were around his grandfather's neck, hugging him tightly. William's whole body ached, but he didn't care. He'd finally found him. He'd found his grandfather!

CHAPTER 40

William gave a jump as he caught sight of a gigantic robot looming over him. This one was even bigger and more threatening than the boar-bot. And instead of a boar's head, the head of a rhino crowned the huge metal body. The robot stood completely still, staring at him with cold eyes, one hand ready to strike.

"Relax. It's deactivated," his grandfather said.

"Deactivated?" William repeated. He looked across at the other containers.

"Lucky that I thawed out before the rest of them. I know where the controls are and I froze them again," his grandfather said, patting the side of Container Number Seven.

They both turned at the sound of a deep rumbling from the hall.

William recognized the sound immediately. It was the big iron door. Someone had opened it.

"Is there anyone else in here?" his grandfather asked him.

"Iscia," William said.

"Iscia?" his grandfather repeated.

"Yes, a girl I know from the Institute," William said.

"You brought someone from the Institute down here?" His grandfather sounded almost angry.

"She helped me," William explained.

His grandfather stormed over to the hole that William had blown in the wall.

"Wait!" yelled William, staggering after him on unsteady legs. "She's on our side."

"I don't believe that for a moment," his grandfather said. The door at the far end of the hall slowly began to open.

A figure stood there, waiting. It was Iscia. William gasped. What was she doing?

"Come on." William's grandfather pulled him along behind him.

"But…" William tried to resist him, but his grandfather was a lot stronger than he looked.

"We don't have much time. Come on!" he said, heading for a hatch at the other end of the room. "We have to get you out of here before they come through."

His grandfather hurried over to the boar-bot, which was lying where it had hit the ground. He pushed some buttons on its back and took a couple of steps backwards. William edged away. The head jerked as the boar-bot opened its eyes and looked around. It spotted William's grandfather and grunted.

"Out there," his grandfather said, pointing back towards

the hall that contained all the vehicles. "Get them."

"No! Wait! Iscia!" William yelled.

But his grandfather wasn't listening. The boar-bot howled and stomped off.

"It should be able to hold them back for a little while." His grandfather frowned as he walked over to a control panel set in the wall beside the hatch and pushed some buttons. There was a gurgling sound that seemed to come from within the walls.

"What's going on?" William cried.

"This is one of the safest bunkers in the world," his grandfather explained. "Soon the whole hall out there will fill with water and they won't be able to get us."

William couldn't believe it. Had his grandfather lost his mind? Or had he always been this crazy? It struck William that he didn't actually know him. He might as well be trapped in here with any random stranger.

"We have to get this open," his grandfather said, heading for a door on the other side of the room.

"Is that an exit?" William asked.

"No, a way deeper into the system." They heard a sound close behind them.

"They're getting nearer," his grandfather muttered, pulling out of his inner jacket pocket something that looked like a pistol. He aimed it at the door. A ball of blue light the size of a tennis ball pulverized the door and the wall around it. A thick cloud of dust filled the room.

"Grandpa?" William yelled.

"Come on!" his grandfather called from somewhere within the cloud of dust.

William pulled his jacket lapel up over his nose, fumbling towards the hole in the wall. There was a tremendous explosion.

The pressure wave was so great that it hurled William through the hole into the darkness.

William landed hard. He lay on his back for a couple of seconds, trying to catch his breath, but the dust made it difficult to breathe.

"Over here!" he heard his grandfather say.

It was too dark to see anything. "Where are we?" he asked.

"We have to get to safety further down," his grandfather said from the darkness. "It's going to take them a while to get past the boar-bot. Follow my voice."

William began to head towards his grandfather, when he felt a hand on his wrist. He tried to prise himself loose, but the grip was too strong.

"Relax," his grandfather said. "It's only me. Come on."

William had no choice but to go where his grandfather led him. Somewhere behind them, he could hear the boar-bot roaring.

They stumbled through the dark until William's grandfather finally came to a halt.

"This is it," William heard him say, followed by a loud *clank* that echoed all around them.

Enormous lamps blinked to life up above, and William stared in astonishment at the sight before him. They were on an old iron scaffold that was attached to the wall of a gigantic grotto. Water was pouring out of several holes in the wall.

"This is—" he began, but he was interrupted by a deep rumble from the darkness behind them.

"They're in. Hurry." His grandfather pulled him down the rusty, swaying metal staircase, heading for the floor of the grotto. "Faster!" his grandfather yelled.

As soon as they reached the ground, William's grandfather turned and gave the brittle staircase a vigorous kick.

The stairs shook, came loose from the rock wall and fell to the ground.

"How are we going to get back up again?" William asked, looking at the rapidly rising water, which was now up to his knees.

"We're not."

"What?" William said.

But his grandfather didn't answer. Instead, his grip tightened round William's wrist.

"WILLIAM!" someone yelled from above.

William looked up and spotted Fritz Goffman leaning over the railing on the scaffolding way above them.

"Run! Get away!" Goffman yelled. "He's not—"

"Don't listen to him, William," his grandfather said. "It's too late, anyway."

William looked at his grandfather. "What do you mean?"

His grandfather didn't respond. He simply stopped, turned and stared at William. There was something menacing in that stare, as if something had come over him. Something dark. William began to panic. The grip around his wrist grew tighter. His hand felt as if it was going to be ripped clean off.

"You're not my grandfather," he said.

The old man sneered. "For one of the brightest boys around, it took you a while to figure that out. Don't you think I deserve an Oscar?" The old man's face twitched into a crooked smile and he let go of William's wrist.

"Who are you?" William asked.

"You have no idea how much I've longed for this," was all the man said.

"Abraham?" William whispered. He felt a chill run down his spine.

"Get away, William!" Goffman yelled. "RUN!"

"But…" William couldn't take his eyes off the old man in front of him. He was transforming right before William's eyes, ageing by the second. His skin was changing colour, blanching until it was almost white.

"Your grandfather was wise to freeze me. Extreme cold is like kryptonite to luridium. But he didn't bank on me thawing faster than him," Abraham said. "And he certainly didn't bank on you being the first one to find us."

"You're full of luridium." William stared at the old man. He couldn't help but be fascinated.

"That's right," snarled Abraham. "And now I need some more." He came closer.

"RUN, WILLIAM!" he heard Iscia scream, but he couldn't move. There was something about the look Abraham was giving him ... it was as if his whole body had turned to ice.

"Where is my grandfather?" William asked.

"He's up there in Number Eight. On his way back to dreamland," Abraham said.

"But why did he freeze himself?" William whispered. He had to know.

"He tricked me down here," Abraham continued. "Said he'd give me the luridium that he'd stolen from the Institute."

"Why would he give you more?" William said.

"Why do you think?" Abraham responded.

William shook his head. His thoughts felt like syrup.

"To prevent me from getting to you," said Abraham. "He did it to save you. Tricked me down here, locked the gates and froze us both. He fooled me. But he didn't count on you coming to save him."

"The hologram!" The words fell out of William's mouth. "It was fake."

"Of course." Abraham smiled. "I still have allies out there. In high places."

Talley came closer, his cold eyes fixed on William. "Do you know how you actually get luridium out of a person's body?" he asked, his voice rising in anticipation.

William gulped and took a few steps back. The water had reached the tops of his thighs now and a strong current was making it difficult for him to stand.

"When the body dies, the luridium's first instinct is to find a new host. So it leaves the body. Choking works best," Abraham said, and raised two sinewy hands. "All I need to do is ... not let go. And the luridium will find me."

"GET AWAY FROM HIM!" William heard Iscia scream. And this time, his body obeyed. Overcome by panic, William turned and began to wade frantically through the water.

"It won't do any good!" he heard Abraham yell after him.

It wasn't easy to get up speed, the water was level with his waist now. But William gritted his teeth and kept going. He wasn't going to give in without a fight. Not even against Abraham Talley.

William quickly glanced up and saw that Iscia, Goffman and the others were all standing on the scaffolding, looking down on the scene unfolding below.

He struggled frantically to keep himself above water. Then he saw a ledge sticking out of the water ahead of him. He scrambled up onto the little shelf, gasping for breath. His body felt completely drained of strength.

"William!" Abraham's voice.

William rolled over and found himself staring right up at Abraham Talley, who had now taken his true form. His skin hung in folds from his face. His head was hairless and his icy eyes flashed. It looked as if he was finally going to get what he'd been waiting for: the luridium that William's grandfather had stolen to save his only grandchild; the luridium that Abraham needed to keep himself alive.

Abraham took a step towards William and planted one foot heavily on his stomach. William could barely breathe.

"Please," he begged.

There was nothing William could do as Abraham leaned over him, placed his bony fingers around William's neck and tightened his grip. Despite his ancient body, he was incredibly strong.

William felt his strength ebbing away. But then a memory popped into his head: the vine that had almost strangled him and the orb that he had used to beat himself free.

Maybe...

William managed to coax the orb out of his jacket pocket and he jabbed it at Abraham's arm.

"Stupid boy." Abraham grinned. "That's not how those things work." He let go of William's neck with one hand and slapped the orb away.

The orb clanked onto the hard stone ledge and rolled away from them. Abraham's free hand returned to William's neck. The skeletal fingers tightened further. William looked up. Iscia and Goffman were still standing on the scaffolding, but the two drivers and Laika were climbing down the wreckage of the rusty staircase. They wouldn't make it in time. William could feel himself starting to drift. Abraham was squeezing the life out of him.

William knew he was giving up.

What could he do against a man who was full of luridium? He felt his body go numb and his consciousness start to fade away. The water was moving up the sides of his face now. Soon he would either be choked or drowned.

But then he felt something. Familiar vibrations in his stomach. The luridium. Of course, Abraham wasn't the only one who was filled with luridium! He was too.

William concentrated on the vibrations. They grew and grew, moving up through his spine and out into his arms. His strength began to return. He opened his eyes and looked at Abraham. It was clear that Talley could sense the power too. There was uncertainty in his eyes now.

"NO!" he snarled. "It belongs to me."

William lifted his arms and grabbed Talley's wrists, gripping them firmly. He focused on the vibrations coursing through his body. As he did, he could feel his own grip tightening and Abraham's fingers loosening.

"Nooooo," Talley hissed. He leaned over William with all his weight and his grasp tightened again. It was like a tug of war between two equally matched teams.

William clenched his teeth and, gathering all his strength, began pulling on Abraham's hands. Slowly he could feel the grip on his neck relaxing. The gnarled fingers were falling away,

Abraham's long fingernails rasping along William's skin in a desperate attempt to keep his grip.

The water had reached the top of William's face now and was flowing into his eyes and nose. He closed his mouth but felt the water entering his lungs with every desperate breath he took. In one final burst of willpower he managed to prise Abraham's hands away. He could see the old man screaming in rage but couldn't hear anything but the sound of the water.

The last thing he saw before his face was fully submerged was Laika lunging at Abraham and sinking her deadly teeth into the nape of the old man's neck.

William must have lost consciousness, because the next thing he knew, he was being carried through the grotto. He caught sight of Iscia and Goffman up ahead and he could see now that it was one of the drivers who was carrying him. They hadn't noticed that he had woken up. William turned his head and saw the other driver with Abraham slung over his shoulder. Was he dead?

William was still dazed and dizzy. He tried to swallow, but his throat was sore from Abraham's grip. He tried to speak, but only a hissing sound came out. The driver carrying him glanced down but continued on. William could hear the splashing of water all around them. This was bad. Very bad.

The little party emerged into the cryogenic chamber and stopped.

"We have to get Tobias out of there," he heard Goffman say.

"And then what? There's no way we'll get out of here before it floods," Iscia said, her voice trembling.

A crazy thought popped into William's head.

"The su—" he began, but he was overcome by a violent coughing seizure.

"He's back!" Iscia cried, hobbling over to him. She stuck her face so close he could feel her breath on his skin and smiled weakly. "You're back," she said.

"The sub..." William tried again.

"What's he saying?" Goffman asked.

"Sub," Iscia said. "What do you mean, William?"

"The subs." William pointed weakly to the chamber outside.

"*The submarines!*" Iscia cried, turning to Goffman. "Do they still work?"

"Only one way to find out," Goffman said. "Which tank is Tobias in?"

"Eight," William mumbled. He could feel himself slipping away again.

"Prise the container loose," William heard Goffman say. "We have to take the whole thing with us."

William tried to stay conscious as Iscia and Goffman carried him out of the cryogenic chamber and into the enormous hall with all the tanks and submarines. Abraham was strapped onto the back of Laika. The two drivers struggled with the large cryogenic container, which must have weighed more than a car. Now the water had reached the hall, and as the small group stopped beside the nearest submarine, it was already up to their knees. The nose of the sub was directed towards a large hole in the wall, which looked like the entrance to a tunnel.

"Is that the only way in?" Iscia asked, looking up at the hatch on top of the submarine.

"Yes," said Goffman.

"How do we get the container right up there?" she said. "And us…?"

"Put me down," said William. The dizziness had passed and he felt stronger now.

Iscia and Goffman carefully helped William to his feet. The water felt cool and refreshing. William looked at the cryogenic container.

"Does it float?" he said. The water was rising fast and was already at his waist.

"It's sealed tight," said Goffman. "To keep the liquid nitrogen inside. So yes, it'll float."

"Then we could use the rising water to get it up there," William suggested.

"Of course!" Goffman shouted and clapped his hands. "We might have a chance after all. Everyone, hold on!"

Minutes later, the rising water had lifted them all to the top of the enormous submarine. The two drivers clambered on and began to turn the large wheel outside the hatch.

"Quickly!" Goffman shouted. "We have to get inside before the water reaches the top."

There was a muffled *clank* from inside the door, and the drivers forced the old hatch up.

"NOW ... we're going to need everyone's help," Goffman called, pulling on the cryogenic container.

As the water reached the open hatch, it started to pour into the submarine, sucking the cryogenic container in through the hole, crashing onto the metal floor below. The rest of the group followed. William was the last one inside. He grabbed the hatch and tried to force it shut. The rush of water was so strong now, it seemed an impossible task, but the drivers came to his rescue. Together they managed to seal it shut.

Soon the group had gathered inside the large control room.

"Now what?" Goffman shouted.

"What about those?" William pointed at two large red levers marked *EJECT*.

"Do it!" Goffman commanded.

William flicked both levers and pulled back. They waited. Nothing happened.

"Do it again!" said Goffman. His voice was trembling now.

William pushed on the levers once more. This time a deep rumble caused the whole submarine to shake.

"That's probably the motors," William whispered.

"Let's hope so," Iscia said as she scanned the cabin warily.

The rumble grew louder. The submarine shook and roared like a space shuttle before it suddenly shot forwards, sending everyone flailing to the floor.

William's arms waved frantically in the air as he tried to grab hold of something.

Anything.

But there was nothing to hang on to. He tumbled backwards and slammed into the wall.

They could hear a loud swishing all around them. It sounded like water rushing past outside the metal hull. Then the gigantic submarine suddenly turned its nose downwards and went into a dive.

William was jolted into the air and then fell back to the floor. He slid forward and caught a glimpse of Iscia, who was clutching a hatch in the wall.

"ISCIA!" William shouted as he carried on past her and crashed into a metal cabinet.

"GRAB HOLD OF SOMETHING!" Goffman's voice called from somewhere in the chaos.

Suddenly it felt as if the whole submarine had tipped backwards and shot up.

William's fingers scraped desperately at the cabin wall in a vain attempt to keep from sliding back again. But it was no use. As the front of the sub shot up, William and the others tumbled backwards and landed in a heap of arms and legs at the end of the control room.

The sound of the water rushing past was so loud now it was no use trying to speak.

William closed his eyes.

For a moment, he thought this was it.

The end.

And then everything went quiet.

He looked up in surprise and saw Iscia squashed up against the wall behind him.

"We've stopped," he said.

"You sure?" Iscia asked.

"Think so." William got to his feet and staggered towards the hatch in the ceiling. Suddenly he had to get out. Had to get air. If there was any out there.

He grabbed the hatch. He must have been full of adrenaline, and much stronger than usual, because the wheel turned easily. He pushed the hatch open.

Bright sunlight and fresh air flooded in from outside. He squinted as he climbed onto the submarine's roof. And took a deep breath.

There was a flashing of bright lights from somewhere near by. Excited voices talking.

He rubbed his eyes, blinked and was surprised to see a boat in front of him. Filled with people. They all had cameras, and they were taking pictures of him. There was something written on the side of the boat: *THAMES TOURS*.

He looked around. There was Big Ben!

The submarine was floating down the middle of the River Thames.

And then he felt it again. The pain in his throat where Abraham had tried to choke him. His legs seemed to disappear from under him.

He fell.

CHAPTER 41

William opened his eyes.

He was lying in a hospital bed hooked up to a web of wires and machines positioned around the bed.

He could hear the sound of a monitor, beeping every time his heart beat. A clear bag with some kind of liquid in it was hanging from a stand next to the bed. A tube ran from the bag into the back of his hand. He tried to swallow. It hurt. He needed some water.

Once his eyes had adjusted to the light, he could see more of the room. He wasn't alone.

Someone was standing over by the window. But he couldn't see who it was. The sunlight was too bright.

"Thirsty…" he said. His voice was hoarse and it hurt to speak. He coughed.

The person turned around and looked at him. "William, you're awake!"

Iscia? William thought.

She was next to the bed in no time, looking down at him and smiling. "How are you feeling?" she said. "You've been in an induced coma for a week."

"Thirsty…" William repeated and started coughing again.

"Of course," Iscia said, hurrying over to a sink in the corner.

She returned to his bedside with a cup. William lifted his head off the pillow and drank.

"My head hurts," he said and put his fingers to his forehead. Iscia pulled a red cord that was hanging on the wall.

"Where am I?" William asked.

"At the Institute," Iscia said.

"I'm not dead?"

"No, but it was close." Iscia grew serious. "Abraham almost managed to get the luridium out of your body."

"The luridium…" William repeated. Everything seemed like a distant nightmare now. "So you know that I have luridium in my body."

"Yes, I know," she said and smiled. "But you're not like the other machines. Even if you are a good deal less human than I thought."

William had to smile. He didn't really know why, but it was nice to hear Iscia say that. They looked at each other for a moment.

Things began to come back to him now.

The submarine.

The River Thames.

"The sub," he said. "It worked."

Iscia smiled again. "If it hadn't been for your idea about that, we'd probably still be down there."

"What about my grandfather?" William asked. Iscia grew sombre.

"Your grandfather is in the isolation ward. They say there's still a chance he'll wake up."

"A chance?" William repeated. "So there's also a chance he might not?"

Iscia looked down. "You'll need to talk to the others," she said.

"I have to see him."

William tried to get up, but collapsed back onto the bed again.

"And Talley…?" he said.

"He's frozen again in an escape-proof container somewhere here at the Institute. I don't think we'll be seeing any more of him," Iscia said. "I don't know much about it, but Goffman said that the luridium in Abraham's body has been in there so long it has absorbed the last of what made him human."

William shrugged. He didn't like the thought of Abraham being at the Institute, but at least they knew where he was now. *And* they could control him.

Iscia hesitated. "There's something I have to tell you," she said finally.

"What?"

"You know my folder? The one I found in the Archive? There was a reason I didn't tell you what was in it – what my job was," she said.

"Why? What was your job?" William asked.

"It was you," she said after a pause.

"Me?"

"Yeah," Iscia said. "My job was to keep an eye on you in case anything happened. And boy, did something happen!"

William lay staring at her.

"That's why you came to find me in London," he said.

"I'm sorry I couldn't tell you the truth. There was too much at stake," she said. "Someone had to be with you in the tunnels."

"I understand." William took her hand.

They looked at each other for a few seconds without speaking. William didn't know what to do now. He didn't know why he'd taken her hand like that. It had just happened. Should he let go and pretend it hadn't, or should he leave his hand there? Both options seemed stupid. He smiled awkwardly. Iscia smiled back.

He quickly pulled his hand away as the door opened and Slapperton dashed into the room. "William," he said once he'd caught his breath. "Uh, I, uh…"

Then the door opened again, and Goffman appeared. He stopped beside Slapperton.

"You're awake," he said.

"Yes," said William.

"I, uh … I…" Goffman continued.

"What they're trying to say is that they're really happy to see you again," Iscia said with a smile. "And they're sorry about everything that's happened."

The two professors blushed.

"Right?" Iscia prompted.

"Erm, yes," they said together.

A few days later, William was buckled into the sofa in the Institute's large plane. He was trembling with excitement. In a couple of hours, he would see his parents again.

It seemed like an eternity since he'd last seen them, and Mr Turnbull, and the rest of the class. So much had happened. He felt like a different person.

A sound from the other end of the cabin made him look up. A figure was approaching. Could it be…?

"Relax, it really is me this time," the figure said and smiled.

"Grandpa?" William said, hesitantly.

His grandfather sat down and studied him for a moment. "You've grown," he observed.

William didn't know what to say. "Thank you…?"

His grandfather laughed. "There's been a bit of improvement since the last time I saw you in the hospital, eight years ago. And you've become a bit of a codebreaker, I hear."

William nodded. "But I think I'm going to take a little

242

break from cryptography for the moment."

His grandfather smiled again and scratched his beard. Then he reached his arm behind his back and scratched there, too. "Sorry. Itchy! Side effect of being frozen for so long. It'll pass eventually."

They sat for a while just looking at each other.

"It's really good to see you again," his grandfather said after a while, almost shyly.

William couldn't help himself any more. He leaped at his grandfather and did something he had dreamed of for as long as he could remember: he flung his arms round his neck and hugged him.

"I thought I would never see you again," William said.

"Me, too," his grandfather said with a crack in his voice.

"What will you do now?" William asked.

"Go home with you and say hello to your parents. I owe them an explanation too," his grandfather said. "Then I'm going to try to convince them to let you come back to the Institute. If you want." His grandfather looked down at William. "Do you?" he said.

There was nothing in the world that William wanted more.

"Absolutely," he said with a grin.

CHAPTER 42

"BREAKFAST!" William's father yelled from downstairs.

William was bent over his desk, working. He peered through a magnifying glass as he tightened a tiny screw into something that looked like a small mechanical beetle.

Then it was his mother's turn. "BREAKFAST!" she hollered.

"Coming!" William replied and put down his screwdriver.

He set the beetle on the desk, looked at it, and smiled. It didn't look quite like the other robot beetle, and he hadn't got it to move yet. But it was a start.

"WILLIAM!" his father yelled.

William got up, grabbed his school backpack and ran out of the room.

Downstairs in the kitchen, everything was as it had always been. His mum and dad were sitting waiting for him at the kitchen table.

"Pancakes," his mum said with a smile. "Even boys who are

only fifty-one per cent human need breakfast, right?"

"Oh, leave the boy alone," his dad said.

"Are you looking forward to going back to school?" his mum asked.

"Not much," William said, rolling up his pancake. He raised it to his mouth and was about to take a bite when a car tooted outside.

"That must be him. He insisted on driving you to school. You'll just have to eat it in the car," his mum said. "Have a good day, darling."

A shiny white car was parked outside.

The back door opened automatically and William hopped in.

"Pancake?" his grandfather said, seeing it rolled up in William's hand. "I love pancakes."

"Do you want it?" William offered.

"No, thanks. I've already eaten."

William cast a glance at the two drivers in the front seat. He still didn't like them. One of them scowled at him in the rearview mirror.

The car began to move off.

"Well, how does it feel?" his grandfather asked, turning to William.

"How does what feel?" William said.

"Not having to live in secrecy any more?"

"It feels good."

"Excellent," his grandfather said.

"Did you get a chance to talk to Mum and Dad about the Institute?" William asked nervously.

"Yes," his grandfather said. "They still need a bit more convincing, but it's all going to work out. I'll make sure it does."

They sat in silence for a few moments.

"But you won't be seeing me for a while," his grandfather said eventually.

"Why not?" William asked. It felt like a blow to his stomach.

"I'm going on a little trip."

"Where to?"

"Tibet."

"Tibet!" William exclaimed. "What are you going to do there?"

"Get something," his grandfather said with a sly smile.

"How long will you be away?"

"I'm not sure. A few weeks, maybe more. We'll see... I think we're here," his grandfather said as the car pulled up outside the school. William's door swung open. His grandfather patted his arm and smiled. "I'm really proud of you, William."

"Thanks," William said, unsure what else to say.

"You'd better hurry. It looks like the bell has already rung," his grandfather said.

William got out of the car but didn't shut the door.

"Was there something else, William?"

"There's something I've been thinking about." William hesitated.

"Yes?"

"If no one could get into that bunker, why was it full of submarines and tanks from the Second World War?"

"That's a very good question, William," his grandfather said with a knowing smile. "Someday I'll tell you. But for now you have to forget all that and concentrate on school, at least for a while. OK?"

"OK," William said, closing the door.

He waved at his grandfather and began to jog towards the school gate. The white Rolls-Royce disappeared around a corner.

Everyone looked up when William walked into the classroom. He stopped next to Mr Turnbull, who was standing at the board with a board rubber in his hand. Mr Turnbull didn't move for a long time, he just stared at him. It seemed as if he was trying to find the right words.

"So your last name is Wenton now?" he finally said. "William Wenton?"

"Yes," said William. "It is."

More adventures from Walker Books...

Collect all the Alex Rider books

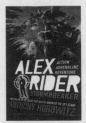

STORMBREAKER

Alex Rider – you're never too young to die…

POINT BLANC

High in the Alps, death waits for Alex Rider…

SKELETON KEY

Sharks. Assassins. Nuclear bombs. Alex Rider's in deep water.

EAGLE STRIKE

Alex Rider has 90 minutes to save the world.

SCORPIA

Once stung, twice as deadly. Alex Rider wants revenge.

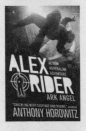

ARK ANGEL

He's back – and this time there are no limits.

SNAKEHEAD

Alex Rider bites back…

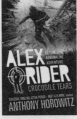

CROCODILE TEARS

Alex Rider – in the jaws of death…

SCORPIA RISING

One bullet. One life. The end starts here.

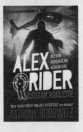

RUSSIAN ROULETTE

Get your hands on the deadly prequel

www.alexrider.com

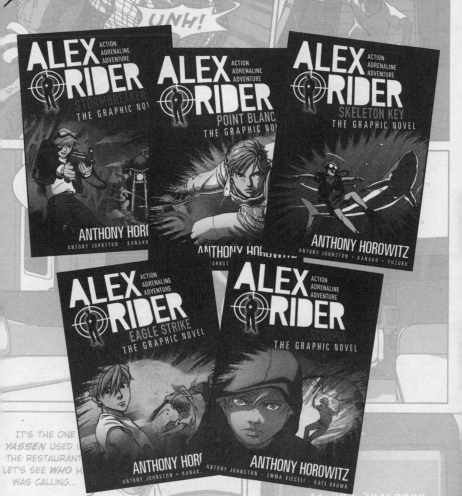

 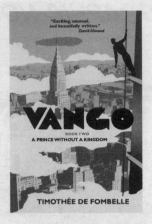

Fleeing from the police and more sinister forces on his trail,
Vango must race against time to prove his innocence.
His journey will take him to the farthest reaches of distant
lands, and even into the sky, where he will find refuge
on board the Graf Zeppelin airship.

**But the threat of war is getting closer, and Vango must
uncover the secrets of his past before everything is lost.**

"Beautiful writing, intricate plotting, and
breathless reveals ... a must-read." *Kirkus*

"A thrilling adventure story ... a distinctive and
atmospherically cinematic tale." *Independent*

JAKE ATLAS

TOMB ROBBER, TREASURE HUNTER, TROUBLEMAKER

A couple of days ago I was a schoolboy with terrible grades
and even worse behaviour – and a way of causing trouble
that drove people nuts.

Now I am a member of a super high-tech treasure-hunting
team searching for a lost tomb so I can save my parents
from being turned into mummies by an evil cult.
Things have moved pretty fast…

Praise for Rob Lloyd Jones's *Wild Boy*:

"Good fun and jolly hair-raising."
The Times

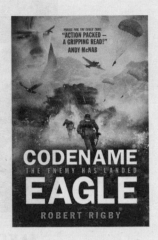

Who is the traitor among us?

Fleeing Nazi-occupied Antwerp, where his father has been shot and his mother arrested, Paul Hansen finds himself in a desperate flight through Belgium and France to the Pyrenees, aided by members of the Resistance.

But the deadliest challenge lies ahead. Does Paul have the wits, strength and will to survive the Eagle Trail?

"Action packed – a gripping read!" Andy McNab

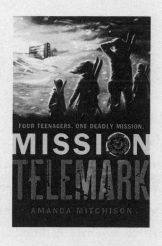

December 1942.

The Nazis occupy Norway. They are on the brink of making the atomic bomb at the power plant at Vemork.

Four teenagers, trained as British Special Operations Agents, are sent on a dangerous mission to destroy the heavily guarded plant.

To succeed, the four must survive the frozen Norwegian wilderness and then outwit the Nazis in a daring act of sabotage. If they fail, Europe faces destruction.

"The plot is fast, the characters engaging and the illustrations and inserts are a brilliant addition … a gripping thriller." *The Scotsman*

Bobbie Peers is an award-winning Norwegian film director and scriptwriter who studied at The London Film School. Peers made his début as a writer for children in 2015 with *Luridiumstyven*, the first in a thrilling adventure series featuring the codebreaking whizz William, which won the Ark Children's Award and the Children's Book Award in its native Norway and is currently shortlisted for the Bokslukerprisen. The book has now been translated into over 30 different languages and is set to become a feature film; it is being published for the first time in English as *William Wenton and the Luridium Thief*, and is in fact the very book you hold in your hands.